THE MAID AND THE MANSION:

AN IMPOSSIBLE HEIST

(The Maid and the Mansion Cozy Mystery—Book Five)

FIONA GRACE

Fiona Grace

Fiona Grace is author of the LACEY DOYLE COZY MYSTERY series, comprising nine books; of the TUSCAN VINEYARD COZY MYSTERY series, comprising seven books; of the DUBIOUS WITCH COZY MYSTERY series, comprising three books; of the BEACHFRONT BAKERY COZY MYSTERY series, comprising six books; of the CATS AND DOGS COZY MYSTERY series, comprising nine books; of the ELIZA MONTAGU COZY MYSTERY series, comprising nine books (and counting); of the ENDLESS HARBOR ROMANTIC COMEDY series, comprising nine books (and counting); of the INN AT DUNE ISLAND ROMANTIC COMEDY series, comprising five books (and counting); of the INN BY THE SEA ROMANTIC COMEDY series, comprising five books (and counting); of the MAID AND THE MANSION COZY MYSTERY series, comprising five books (and counting); of the ALICE BLOOM COZY MYSTERY series, comprising five books (and counting).

Fiona would love to hear from you, so please visit www.fionagraceauthor.com to receive free ebooks, hear the latest news, and stay in touch.

BOOKS BY FIONA GRACE

THE MAID AND THE MANSION COZY MYSTERY
A MYSTERIOUS MURDER (Book #1)
A SCANDALOUS DEATH (Book #2)
A MISSING GUEST (Book #3)
AN UNSOLVABLE CRIME (Book #4)
AN IMPOSSIBLE HEIST (Book #5)

INN BY THE SEA ROMANTIC COMEDY
A NEW LOVE (Book #1)
A NEW CHANCE (Book #2)
A NEW HOME (Book #3)
A NEW LIFE (Book #4)
A NEW ME (Book #5)

THE INN AT DUNE ISLAND ROMANTIC COMEDY
A CHANCE LOVE (Book #1)
A CHANCE FALL (Book #2)
A CHANCE ROMANCE (Book #3)
A CHANCE CHRISTMAS (Book #4)
A CHANCE ENGAGEMENT (Book #5)

ENDLESS HARBOR ROMANTIC COMEDY
ALWAYS, WITH YOU (Book #1)
ALWAYS, FOREVER (Book #2)
ALWAYS, PLUS ONE (Book #3)
ALWAYS, TOGETHER (Book #4)
ALWAYS, LIKE THIS (Book #5)
ALWAYS, FATED (Book #6)
ALWAYS, FOR LOVE (Book #7)
ALWAYS, JUST US (Book #8)
ALWAYS, IN LOVE (Book #9)

ELIZA MONTAGU COZY MYSTERY
MURDER AT THE HEDGEROW (Book #1)
A DALLOP OF DEATH (Book #2)
CALAMITY AT THE BALL (Book #3)

A SPEAKEASY DEMISE (Book #4)
A FLAPPER FATALITY (Book #5)
BUMPED BY A DAME (Book #6)
A DOLL'S DEBACLE (Book #7)
A FELLA'S RUIN (Book #8)
A GAL'S OFFING (Book #9)

LACEY DOYLE COZY MYSTERY
MURDER IN THE MANOR (Book#1)
DEATH AND A DOG (Book #2)
CRIME IN THE CAFE (Book #3)
VEXED ON A VISIT (Book #4)
KILLED WITH A KISS (Book #5)
PERISHED BY A PAINTING (Book #6)
SILENCED BY A SPELL (Book #7)
FRAMED BY A FORGERY (Book #8)
CATASTROPHE IN A CLOISTER (Book #9)

TUSCAN VINEYARD COZY MYSTERY
AGED FOR MURDER (Book #1)
AGED FOR DEATH (Book #2)
AGED FOR MAYHEM (Book #3)
AGED FOR SEDUCTION (Book #4)
AGED FOR VENGEANCE (Book #5)
AGED FOR ACRIMONY (Book #6)
AGED FOR MALICE (Book #7)

DUBIOUS WITCH COZY MYSTERY
SKEPTIC IN SALEM: AN EPISODE OF MURDER (Book #1)
SKEPTIC IN SALEM: AN EPISODE OF CRIME (Book #2)
SKEPTIC IN SALEM: AN EPISODE OF DEATH (Book #3)

BEACHFRONT BAKERY COZY MYSTERY
BEACHFRONT BAKERY: A KILLER CUPCAKE (Book #1)
BEACHFRONT BAKERY: A MURDEROUS MACARON (Book #2)
BEACHFRONT BAKERY: A PERILOUS CAKE POP (Book #3)
BEACHFRONT BAKERY: A DEADLY DANISH (Book #4)
BEACHFRONT BAKERY: A TREACHEROUS TART (Book #5)
BEACHFRONT BAKERY: A CALAMITOUS COOKIE (Book #6)

CATS AND DOGS COZY MYSTERY

A VILLA IN SICILY: OLIVE OIL AND MURDER (Book #1)
A VILLA IN SICILY: FIGS AND A CADAVER (Book #2)
A VILLA IN SICILY: VINO AND DEATH (Book #3)
A VILLA IN SICILY: CAPERS AND CALAMITY (Book #4)
A VILLA IN SICILY: ORANGE GROVES AND VENGEANCE
(Book #5)
A VILLA IN SICILY: CANNOLI AND A CASUALTY (Book #6)

ALICE BLOOM COZY MYSTERY
MURDER IN THE MARIGOLDS (Book #1)
RUIN IN THE ROSES (Book #2)
DECEIT IN THE DAFFODILS (Book #3)
SCANDAL IN THE SAFFRON (Book #4)
CATASTROPHE IN THE CARNATIONS (Book #5)

CHAPTER ONE

The sweet smell of rich, sugary berry jam on the boil wafted outside, from the big kitchen window, to where Mary Adams was sweeping the courtyard. The courtyard contained several large pots of herbs and had a panoramic view of the berry orchards on the hillside.

Seven weeks ago, when she started work at Beaumont Place, working for the wealthy, but kindly-natured, Lady Beaumont, Mary would have associated this smell and sight with the lighthearted freedom of summer.

But now, as she breathed in the aroma and stared out over the neat rows of berry bushes, she couldn't prevent a frisson of nervousness.

This was no ordinary jam. It represented the pinnacle of Lady Beaumont's tireless work and talent, as well as the entire estate's hopes and dreams.

Over the past weeks, Mary had watched the berries ripen on the lovingly tended vines, planted in neat rows on the sunniest slopes of the hillside, in fertile yet well drained soil. Then, she had watched the regal, gray-haired widow herself head out with a basket in her hand, in the evening just before sundown, and hand pick the choicest of the crop, carefully washing each berry in the large sink outside the kitchen.

Now, the finishing touches were being made to what would hopefully be the prizewinning jam at the Oaktree Village Summer Gathering. But the problem was that Lady Beaumont seemed uncharacteristically nervous. Over the past few days, she'd been brittle, tense and snappish. In fact, she'd turned into a completely different person from the one who'd welcomed Mary and Hannah to the estate in late spring, in a calm and friendly way, while explaining their duties as the stand-in housemaids for two employees who were taking eight weeks of long leave.

Then, the household had seemed like a calm, happy place. Now, Mary was feeling more and more frequently as if she were walking on eggshells.

Was Lady Beaumont always like this when the pressure intensified, Mary wondered. Perhaps it was due to pre-competition nerves.

Or was there a problem with the jam this time around – one which might cost the estate this prestigious title?

"If you could fetch me the butter?" The lady's sharp, clear voice rang out, causing Mary to turn her head in the other direction, this time toward the kitchen window.

Was she talking to Mary?

Deciding it was better to be sure, because the timing might be critical, Mary propped her broom against the white-painted wall. Eager to help, she rushed through the kitchen door, smoothing down her gray apron and tucking back a lock of her butter-blond hair that had been blown loose by the summer breeze.

Hurrying through the scullery, which was neat and clean, with a pile of dried dishes on the side table ready to put back into the cupboard, she headed into the spacious and modern kitchen, where the aroma of the jam simmering on the big electric stove was intense, almost overpowering.

Wielding a long spoon, with her hair tied back and covered by a silken headscarf, the tall, rangy widow was lightly caressing the surface of the jam with the tip of the spoon.

"Almost ready," she muttered, without even looking up. Her attention was entirely focused on her sweet, fruity creation.

And her instruction hadn't been for Mary. In fact, Mary's best friend Hannah was already returning from the pantry, with the block of butter on a tray.

Hannah gave Mary an excited glance, her brown eyes sparkling.

"Doesn't it smell delicious?" she said in encouraging tones, putting the butter down within easy reach of Lady Beaumont, on the counter beside the stove.

"It smells mouthwatering," Mary agreed supportively.

"I'm not sure about the consistency," Lady Beaumont muttered to herself, shaking her head, still keeping her gaze fixed on the pot. "It might cool perfectly, but it might be a touch too runny. At least the butter will make the consistency glossy. But now – do I boil it again or not?"

Sighing, she stared down. Her shoulders looked tense. She was gripping the spoon – hard.

This meant everything to her, Mary realized, with a twist of her stomach. It was far more than just bringing home a trophy.

To add to the pressure, Mary knew this was the last batch that she'd have time to make before the fair, which was tomorrow. Although the three previous batches had seemed perfect to her, Lady Beaumont had found minor flaws with them. But there wasn't time to make any more. The limiting factor seemed to be the berries themselves, which had taken longer than usual to ripen, thanks to a rainy spell and some unseasonably cold weather in early June.

Lady Beaumont spooned a tablespoon of the jam into a saucer. This was the fourth saucer she'd used so far. She waited, peering down at the saucer, prodding it with her spoon.

"Should it go through one more boil?" the lady asked. "What do I need to do to make it perfect? How do I retain my title this year? What will *he* like?"

That last question was uttered in stressed, brittle tones.

"Does the temperature of the kitchen make a difference to the jam?" Mary asked. She had no idea if this was a factor or not. All she was trying to do was to offer some constructive input. However, to her shock, Lady Beaumont reacted in a most uncharacteristic way.

She turned – ripping her gaze from the jam for the first time in hours – and glared at Mary.

"Do you have any practical experience of jam making?"

Shocked, Mary took a step back. She hadn't expected an attack, and the tone in Lady Beaumont's voice was vitriolic.

This was showing a new side of her, one that Mary had never known existed.

"No, ma'am, I don't have any experience at all of jam making. I was just hoping to learn more about it," she said humbly.

"Ah." Lady Beaumont nodded, breathing out, grimacing as if she was forcing herself back into a better temper. "Well, the ambient temperature shouldn't make a difference at this stage. If the jam was being made in a freezing kitchen or in a massive heat wave, then it might be a factor when doing the saucer test. But since jam is made in summer, freezing temperatures are never likely. And berries are best not picked in a heat wave in any case."

Her voice was warmer now, and Mary breathed a sigh of relief as she nodded, smiling at her employer.

"That's so interesting. I must say, good jam is such a delight to eat. One of my favorite foods. So simple and yet so versatile," she enthused.

"Bread, toast, scones, pastries, jam makes them all," Hannah added.

Mary knew that her friend had sensed that flare-up and was also working hard to improve the lady's mood.

"I'm not an expert, but to me, your jam is the best I've ever tasted. It's not only the flavor, but the consistency, and the amount of fruit. I've had a whole new appreciation for it since working here."

Lady Beaumont turned to Mary with an approving smile at those words of praise, before refocusing once more on her test saucer, glancing indecisively at the butter as if wondering whether it was the right time to commit to adding it.

Feeling as if she could contribute no more, Mary headed back outside to finish her sweeping.

But the scathing tone in Lady Beaumont's voice as she'd lashed out at her still rankled, and as she picked up her broom again, she realized Lady Beaumont was definitely bitter at times.

Perhaps that was because she had lost the love of her life, Lord Beaumont, during the war. Since she'd been working at Beaumont Place, Mary had learned that Lord Beaumont had been a general, and had died in an aerial attack while leading an invasion in Germany. That had been just two and a half years ago.

It made her feel deeply troubled to think of this tragedy. After twenty-five years of marriage, Lady Beaumont was now alone, apart from one son.

Mary had no idea what it must feel like to lose such a loved partner. The idea filled her with horror, all the more so because until recently, she hadn't known what it was like to have a loved partner.

But after the holiday she'd had before starting work here, she thought she understood what love was. Gilbert MacLeod, the man she'd met by chance while working at her first housemaid's job, had taken her and Hannah away for a few days by the seaside, and what an experience it had been.

For Mary, the swishing of the waves and the smell of the sea, the misting of the spray on her face and the soft squish of sand under her toes, would be forever linked with the memories of Gilbert. His smile, his sense of fun, the time they'd raced each other down the stretch of beach, the times they'd kissed.

Over those blissful three days of holiday, it had become very clear to her that Gilbert was the man for her, but the situation wasn't so simple. Life didn't seem to be allowing them to spend time together. Summer was the busiest time for Gilbert, who had started a business selling hybrid seeds to farmers, and he was currently traveling to a different part of the country every week. Even exchanging fond letters, which had saved her sanity, was not easy when the object of the fondness was in a different place every couple of days.

Thankfully, he was now based at a hotel about a hundred miles south of where she was now, for a few days. She planned to write to him first thing tomorrow, and would definitely include the story of the jam making.

Finishing her sweeping, Mary tapped the broom on the edge of the stair to clean it, before heading back inside. The smell of the jam reminded her of the pressure Lady Beaumont was under.

She hoped that nothing would go wrong tomorrow, at the Oaktree Village summer gathering, when the jams were finally judged. The problem was that a few days ago, Mary had accidentally discovered something kept secret by Lady Beaumont, that had made her realize victory was not certain.

Never before had she known that Lady Beaumont possessed such an angry side. And if she lost the competition, Mary now feared what might happen if it was unleashed.

CHAPTER TWO

Heading upstairs to collect the used tea trays from the sunny second floor parlor, Mary couldn't help giving a concerned glance into the small annex that Lady Beaumont used as a study.

And of course, once she'd glanced inside, she could not stop herself from detouring into the room. This was where she'd discovered the secret that Lady Beaumont didn't know she knew about.

A few days ago, when cleaning the study, Mary had accidentally jostled a folder that had been left open on the desk. Her movement had caused a few of the pages inside to fall out. Annoyed by her own clumsiness, she'd hastily gathered them up and put them back, as close to the way she'd found them as she'd been able to manage.

The problem was that she'd ended up glancing at the pages themselves while she did this. Not intentionally, of course, but she was a keen reader, and it was hard not to read newspaper clippings when they were right in front of your eyes.

The series of clippings were fairly recent, dating from a few weeks ago, back to a year ago. And all of them were related to the growers of fruit and the makers of jam who lived in the Oaktree district.

Now, opening the folder again, Mary reread the articles, feeling her worries surge.

"Samuel Blackthorn is Lauded as the Marmalade Maker of the Future," read one. Another blared out, "Lady Rotherham Praises Latest Cherry Harvest as Best Yet for Preserves," and another read, "New Jam Making Techniques Set Mrs. Pringle's Local Creations Apart."

All these crafters were going to prove a threat at the actual event. Mary knew it with a cold certainty. The competition was by no means a guaranteed win, and if Lady Beaumont was going to retain her title, then she'd better have made sure that the consistency of the jam was perfection itself.

Sighing, knowing that she couldn't be more anxious about the outcome, Mary tried to put her worries aside as she closed the folder and headed into the parlor. There, the head housekeeper, a matronly woman of about thirty-five years old, was busy with the long feather duster that had to be used to keep the room's high corners spiderweb-free.

"Ah, Mary," she said in kindly tones. "Wouldn't you take this tea set downstairs to be washed? And I meant to tell you, there's another one in the summerhouse. Lady Beaumont had some friends over for lunch, and I believe they're in town now, but coming back for dinner. And also, won't you put some fresh flowers into the first spare bedroom?"

"I'll do all that," Mary said. "Who's arriving?"

So far, Lady Beaumont had not been much of a one for socializing. Mary had worked at many homes where the guest bedrooms were as busy as country hotels in high season. No sooner had one set of guests left than another arrived. But Lady Beaumont had kept to herself so far, which made the arrival of a guest more intriguing.

The housekeeper moved to the next corner and wielded the duster again, fluffing it into the corner.

"It's the lady's son who'll be arriving," she said. "Maxwell Beaumont."

There was something in the way she said the name that had Mary frowning. It sounded as if the head housekeeper, who'd never seemed to hold a grudge against anybody, was prejudiced against the arriving son.

"And does he ever cause problems?" Mary asked, feeling that if there was going to be trouble, she at least needed to know.

"He's just a little… strange," the housekeeper admitted. "Impulsive, you know? Sometimes he speaks before he thinks. But he's done well for himself, I believe, made himself a pile of money. A clever man, that's for sure."

"He has?" Mary felt surprised. She was used to upper class employers inheriting their fortunes. But there were exceptions, and Gilbert came immediately to her mind.

Gilbert wasn't strictly speaking upper class – his father had made a fortune selling affordable furniture, and had then bought an estate that somebody had been desperate to sell. And she knew of a few others who'd done likewise.

"What does Maxwell do?" she asked.

The housekeeper shrugged. "Something to do with stocks and trades. I'll admit, I don't understand it at all. It's a risky business, you know, and easy to lose everything. I must say, I've wondered about him in the past and the company he keeps." Catching herself, she shook her head as if angry she'd let herself gossip. "But I will say, I admire him for not relying on his inheritance the way so many others do," she said firmly.

Mary could see she was trying hard to speak well of her employer's son.

"I'll make sure that the room has the nicest flowers I can find," she promised. Taking the tea tray, she hurried out. She retraced her route back to the kitchen, put the tea tray in the sink, and then headed outside with a pair of shears, to cut some of the prettiest blooms, ready for arrangement in Maxwell's room.

Some of these delightful carnations, in red and white, would be perfect, Mary decided. Bright and bold, they would add a pleasing splash of color to the room, especially since that guest bedroom had hints of red in its décor.

A touch of greenery was essential in a flower vase, too. Some of these leaves would work well, and perhaps a few of these daisies, just for a pleasing contrast in the size of the blooms. Snipping away, she wielded the shears.

With her posy ready, she headed back inside to hunt for a vase. Finding a suitable one, made of simple white china, Mary arranged the flowers inside, added water, and then carried it up the stairs to the spare bedroom.

She placed them on the dressing table and did one final check, making sure the room was in pristine condition for this important guest. Everything looked perfect. The bedcovers were smooth, the cushions on the leather armchair were plumped, even the fringes of the rug on the floor looked neatly aligned.

As she hurried out of the bedroom and back down the corridor, she heard the wheels of a car, scrunching on the gravel drive outside, and the click of the latch as the butler opened the front door. Their problem guest, who kept dubious company, had arrived.

"Welcome, Master Beaumont," she heard the butler say, as she rounded the corner.

"Hope I'm not too late for dinner," a drawling voice replied. "It's been a tough day in the markets."

"Dinner will be served in an hour," the butler replied.

"My dearest Maxwell. You made it in time!"

Lady Beaumont's voice held no trace of the sternness that she'd used earlier when addressing Mary about the jam. It was clear that she adored her son.

"An hour? I'd like dinner sooner than that. I'm starving," Maxwell announced.

"We'll fix it for earlier, then. Come and have a gin and tonic," Lady Beaumont urged him. "I'm so glad you're here. I've been getting nervous about tomorrow."

"What's happening tomorrow?" Maxwell asked.

"It's the summer gathering, of course. And the jam competition."

As the two of them headed into the parlor where the butler awaited with the drinks trolley, Mary clearly heard Maxwell's next words.

"You don't have a thing to worry about, mother. Your jam is going to be the clear winner. And if anyone dares to go up against you – I know for a fact they'll pay the price."

There was something in his tone that made Mary shiver. But there wasn't time now to wonder about what he might have meant.

While the butler took the suitcases up to the spare bedroom, Mary rushed to the kitchen. Dinner served sooner than planned meant a massive rush. The cook and the two assistants were already bustling around.

"The crusty bread! Is it ready?" the cook asked.

"It should be baked in another twenty minutes." The assistant, adjusting his chef's hat, quickly checked the oven.

"Guess that'll have to do. And the fresh asparagus? Has that been washed?"

"I'll attend to that," Mary called, making a beeline for the green, lush pile of asparagus that had been freshly picked just that afternoon from the estate's sizeable vegetable garden.

"We'll have it lightly steamed, with a simple lemon butter sauce," the cook called, and Mary felt pleased that the cook clearly trusted her with this food preparation without looking over her shoulder.

She had some hard-earned experience working in kitchens in previous jobs, and always felt it was one of the more fun parts of service. After all, a beautifully made bed was all well and good, but it didn't delight guests the way a steaming venison pie with a rich red wine sauce, or a fluffy chocolate mousse with whipped cream and a cherry on top, did!

Mary rinsed the asparagus and placed it in a sieve over steaming water, while Hannah rushed to help with the main course, which was venison – tender slices of loin, accompanied by summer peas, and boiled baby potatoes with lashings of butter.

For dessert, Lady Beaumont had opted for the simple, yet seasonal, choice of strawberry ice cream, made with fresh crushed strawberries and the finest fresh cream.

Dinner service was always an activity that demanded the utmost focus, which Mary enjoyed. Sometimes, especially when she had worries on her mind, her own thoughts could run away with her if she let them. Right now, with service on the go and the need to juggle every element of the dinner to perfection, there wasn't time to worry about anything else.

Not the angry tone that Lady Beaumont had used earlier, not the fact that she hadn't had a letter from Gilbert in the past two days, not the fact that she needed to think about her own future seriously.

When the two permanent housemaids were back at work again, she and Hannah would be jobless once more, and it would be time for Mary to do some serious thinking about her own future.

There was a big decision to be made, and she had no idea what to do about it. She had to admit that the thought of her own future was causing her a lot of stress. It felt like there was an unsolved dilemma looming, and the more she worried about it, the less she knew what the right decision would be.

"Now, Mary!" The cook's voice cut into her thoughts. "What are you doing? You just took the meat out of the oven to rest. Why are you putting it back again?"

"Sorry!" Flushing in confusion, she let go of the plate and took off her oven gloves, but the cook continued to stare at her.

"You've got something worrying you, haven't you? I can tell. We're all troubled in this house at the moment, with this competition coming up, and Lady Beaumont behaving so erratically, not to mention the arrival of her problem son, but this is something different, isn't it?"

"It is," Mary admitted. The cook was right.

"What is it?" she asked.

Mary took a deep breath. Her future was at stake here, and maybe getting a stranger's opinion would be a good idea.

"I'm in a spot of bother," she admitted. "If you've got a minute to listen, I'll tell you all about it."

CHAPTER THREE

Mary glanced at the cook inquiringly, not wanting to burden the woman with her own problems, but at the same time, feeling grateful for her kindness in asking.

Looking curious, the cook nodded. "I have a minute," she agreed.

"Well, you see," Mary said, "when this job ends, and when Lady Beaumont's full time maids are back from their leave, I need to decide what to do next."

"Aye, that's a challenge. Jobs are scarce these days," the cook said sympathetically, ladling gravy into the jug as Mary sprinkled parsley over the boiled potatoes.

"I have two choices. The first one is to look for another housemaid's job, together with my friend, Hannah."

The cook nodded. "You're both good workers," she said in a reserved way.

"The problem is," Mary confessed, "that I've unfortunately had some – some trouble associated with me, in previous positions."

"And that I've also heard about," the cook said. "News travels fast, you know. I know well that you've been involved in trouble. In fact, the head housekeeper at your previous place of work warned me that Mary Adams always seems to end up in sticky situations, even though they're not of her own making."

Mary nodded humbly. The world was small when it came to things like murders being committed at grand estates. People talked, and word got around, and that was when employers got nervous. Nobody liked hiring trouble.

"Yes. I know that's going to be a challenge if I look for another job," Mary admitted.

"Well, there's been no trouble here, has there? So far, anyway. Maybe that means your run of bad luck is over," the cook said optimistically. "But what's the other choice?"

"The other choice is a more unpredictable one. It's working for a private detective. He needs an assistant. He works throughout England, and obviously, it would be a more erratic job."

"And more dangerous, surely?" Staring at her, spoon in hand, the cook asked that difficult question.

"Well, riskier than being a housemaid, yes," Mary admitted.

The cook sighed. "Seems you've got some difficult choices ahead of you, Mary Adams. You've got to decide whether or not to make a big change in your life. That's not easy to have to do. And you don't have much time to decide. These two maids should be back in a week or two. But for now, I need you to focus on the job at hand. Save the worrying for – for when you're on a morning walk. I've seen you out there, walking in the early mornings."

"I love to walk," Mary admitted with a smile, realizing that from the cook's standpoint, this conversation was now over, even though her own dilemma was still not resolved.

If she took the job with the private detective, where would she base herself? Would she rent a flat or share a house with somebody? If Hannah took another job, then Mary's best friend would be live-in – after all, that was the nature of the housemaids' world – and that might mean she and Hannah would have to part ways.

There were so many decisions to make in her future, that it was far easier simply to arrange the slices of venison on the plates, nestle the peas in a pile next to the potatoes, and make sure that the gravy was generously, yet artistically, poured onto the plate.

"Mmm, it smells good," Hannah said, arriving at the serving station, ready to take the plates through to the guests. "I think everyone will enjoy this."

"I hope so," Mary said. "I don't know that Lady Beaumont has much of an appetite tonight because she's so nervous about the outcome of the jam competition tomorrow. But at least her friends, and her son, will eat well."

She took two plates through to the dining room, where Lady Beaumont was sitting at one end of the table, with her son at her right hand side, and three other guests making up the numbers.

Mary hadn't yet seen Maxwell Beaumont. She stole a glance at him as she was setting the plates down.

Her first impression was that this son was not a likeable person. He had a sulky mouth and his face seemed set in a permanent frown. He'd inherited Lady Beaumont's sharp features, but without the hint of regal beauty that gave the lady her class.

"The trading's been taking all my time," he was explaining to one of the other guests, holding out his wineglass for a butler to refill it.

"It's a very complex process, you know. Ordinary people can't do it. They can't even understand it."

He said the words in a rather disparaging way, as if the guest who'd asked was automatically classed as one of the 'ordinary people', and would therefore be ignorant.

"I see," the woman who was conversing with Maxwell said, with a polite but confused smile, as the butler moved to her with the bottle. "I'd like to try to understand, though."

"Some other time," Maxwell said with a sigh that made Mary bristle, because there was something disparaging about both the action and his expression.

"Do you ever lose money on it?" the man sitting across the table from Maxwell challenged him.

Mary saw Maxwell flinch noticeably. "Lose money? Of course not. I never lose my clients' money!"

"Oh, really? So if we invested, say, two thousand pounds with you, what would happen if we needed it a month or two down the line?"

"You'd get it back, of course. Don't you believe I'm honest?"

Suddenly, there was a charged atmosphere around the dinner table. Maxwell had flushed deep red. The guest across the table was leaning forward, staring at him intensely. Lady Beaumont was looking from one to the other in concern.

"All I'm asking is a simple question," the neighbor said. "Why is it making you so angry?"

"Well, to give you a short answer, then yes. You'd get the money back, even though it's all invested in trades for a certain period. I'd pay you myself."

"Hmmm," the neighbor said, dubiousness audible in his tone.

Mary set the plates down without a word and turned away, feeling glad to be walking out of that surprisingly tense environment and back into the kitchen.

Now, it was time to take the ice cream out of the freezer, so that it had a chance to melt just a little, and to get as creamy and silken as it could be. The ice cream would be topped with chopped strawberries that had been soaked in a creamy liquor and finished off with a sprinkling of mint. The bowls, as Mary prepared them carefully, looked a picture. She wished she actually owned a camera, so that she could take a photograph of the beautiful and sumptuous looking desserts, in their blue and white bowls.

In no time at all, the dessert was being served, and Mary was rinsing off the dinner plates. With the service now almost over, she could finally relax. The kitchen maids would finish off the remainder of the work, and she and Hannah could head to the pantry and get some leftovers for their dinner.

"I must say," Hannah whispered, as they headed through to the staff pantry, "I didn't think that Maxwell Beaumont was a particularly likable man. He seemed to have a superior attitude, if you ask me. And why was that neighbor so suspicious of him? There seemed to be a reason."

Mary nodded. "I also picked that suspicion up. Maxwell definitely had an oversized ego, and was being rude to that man's wife. Maybe that's why he challenged him."

"I wonder how much money he's really making," Hannah said.

"You mean he could be in financial difficulty?" Mary asked.

Hannah shrugged. "What do you think?"

Now that Hannah had put the idea into her head, Mary was wondering.

Maybe Maxwell had been too defensive, a sure sign of guilt in Mary's experience. Or the neighbor knew something that Maxwell hadn't wanted to be common knowledge.

"At least all that conversation must have taken Lady Beaumont's mind off the summer gathering tomorrow," Hannah observed. "She didn't have time to mention the competition."

"Well, Maxwell made that easy. Instead of worrying about the jam, she was fretting about her son instead?" Mary asked.

"Oh, poor Lady Beaumont!" Hannah ran her hands through her hair. "Shall I make us sandwiches with two slices of this venison, and the rest of the bread?"

"Thanks," Mary said.

At that moment, thinking of leftovers and dirty dishes, she gave a horrified gasp. In the excitement of Maxwell's arrival, she'd completely forgotten to do one of the important jobs she'd been asked to do earlier.

"I've got to run outside quickly," she said. "I'll be back in five minutes. I realized I forgot to take the dirty teacups back from the summerhouse."

Berating herself for having been absentminded and distracted, Mary hurried out of the pantry, headed through the kitchen door, and followed the narrow, slate-paved pathway that led on a winding route to the summer house. It was now after nine p.m., and fully dark.

But, as she walked, she picked up on another set of footsteps treading down the driveway to the main gate, and turned to stare, curiously.

In the faint gleam of moonlight, she saw a man, dressed in a dark jacket, was heading up to the estate's gate, where Mary now saw the headlights of a car were waiting.

It took her another moment to realize that the figure was Maxwell. He must have excused himself from after-dinner drinks, and be heading up to the gate to speak to someone. That was all well and good, but something about his demeanor, the stealthy way he was walking, the glance over his shoulder, told Mary that he clearly didn't want anyone to know where he was going.

Was this a secret meeting?

Puzzled and suspicious, she tiptoed behind him, wondering if she could get a clearer idea of what he was doing, without being discovered herself. She froze as Maxwell looked around once more, pressing herself against the hedge and lowering her head so that the white blur of her face wouldn't be visible, only her dark cap.

After a seemingly endless pause, where Mary expected him to shout out and ask her what she was doing, Maxwell continued to the gate.

She didn't dare walk any further in that direction. The grassy border between the hedge and the driveway narrowed here, and if she stepped onto the gravel, then the crunch of her footsteps would alert him. But as Maxwell approached the car, she heard voices – too low for her to be able to figure out what was being said, though.

Maxwell was speaking to another man, and it was clearly a secretive issue, from the murmur of the voices. But then, suddenly, they rose, and she heard one of the men give a quick, angry shout.

Her blood chilled. Which of them was shouting, and why? What was this all about? There had been real fury in that tone. Whatever this meeting had been about, it had ended acrimoniously. And that meant it would be far wiser for her to disappear.

Quickly, she turned and crept back along the grass, heading for the summerhouse to get that tea tray.

She felt deeply concerned as she took the tray back to the manor house. There had been nothing innocent about that strange and furtive meeting.

She had a strong feeling that she wasn't the only one attracting unwanted trouble. The dislikeable Maxwell seemed to be inviting it right up to the gates of Beaumont Place.

CHAPTER FOUR

As strains of music gusted on the summer breeze, and the sun blazed down from a cloudless sky, the serene environment was soothing the trepidation Mary had felt last night. On such a glorious summer's day, it seemed impossible that anything should go wrong.

With the village green just half a mile from Beaumont Place, Lady Beaumont had kindly given most of the staff the day off to enjoy the summer gathering. Mary and Hannah had walked there together.

It was a quick and easy walk along the cobbled road that led into the village. The road sloped slightly downhill, giving them a view of the village green as they headed toward it.

"Doesn't it all look pretty?" Hannah exclaimed.

The well mowed green, studded with hazel trees, was a hive of colorful activity. Several tents and stalls had been set up, the band was playing, and the village streets were already lined with cars. This event was attracting a lot of out-of-towners. For today, the village was the destination of choice for everyone in the county, it seemed.

"I do love hearing a trumpet in a band," Hannah said, grinning as she tilted her head to take in the tuneful sounds.

"I do love cotton candy, and look, they're selling sticks at that stall near the entrance," Mary said.

A poster at the main entrance advertised all the gathering's attractions.

"Food Stalls, Crafts and Other Creations. Live Music. The Famous Oaktree Village Produce Competition – Best Jam, Best Flower Arrangement, Best Cake. Final Jam Judging at 4 p.m."

She and Hannah paid their shilling's entrance fee, which entitled them to two drinks vouchers, and headed through the archway of twined branches, decorated with flowers, that formed the gathering's temporary gateway.

"Cotton candy first?" Mary pleaded, making a beeline for the stall, and standing in line, watching as the attendant wrapped a stick in a gauzy, colorful layer of the spun sugar.

She simply loved cotton candy! She paid for a stick for herself and for Hannah, and they headed into the fairgrounds.

There was a lot more going on than she'd seen from up on the hill. There were toffee apples for sale, and there was a coconut-shy stall that had some great prizes on offer. There was even a maze, made from straw bales, that you navigate, with prizes for the best time through, and Mary knew as soon as she saw it that she simply had to try that challenge.

There were pony rides and carriage rides, and there were some fun races being organized. A sack race, a three legged race, an egg and spoon race. Schoolchildren were lining up for the egg and spoon race, glancing at each other in a competitive way.

There was a bar, which was already doing a lively trade in gin and tonics, even at this early hour of the morning, and there was a food kiosk that was serving delicious looking mini chicken pies, fruit sticks, sausage rolls, and cheese sandwiches.

There was so much color, and sound, and activity, that Mary felt positively enthralled as she wove her way between the stalls, where it seemed you could buy anything you wanted to.

"Kitchen tools for sale! Labor saving inventions!" A pink cheeked man, with a label on his jacket that named him as Donald Watson, was standing in front of a kiosk with well stocked shelves. "Make this summer a time to relax! Come and look at our easy to use egg beaters, and our fabulous new irons, our vacuum cleaners for a spotless home, and take a look at the latest model of electrical stove! We can order yours, and prepare you for a life of luxury!"

Quite a few women were clustered around the stand, looking interestedly at the various appliances.

Moving on, Mary realized it wouldn't be a country event without horsy items for sale.

"Daniel Moore's Fine Saddlery" advertised the next stall. Mary wasn't a horse rider, but she could only admire the fine leather, the beautifully stitched headcollars and blankets, and the saddles, made from such high quality leather that it practically glowed. Mr. Moore himself, a man in his fifties with a weathered face and a pragmatic air about him, was busy showing off a selection of saddles to a customer in a riding jacket.

"Now, this is interesting!" Hannah had wandered ahead to the next stall. Turning, she beckoned to Mary to catch up.

"Buy a Piece of Paradise from George Hopkins Estates," the stall advertised. A man with well-cut, wavy dark hair, wearing an immaculately tailored jacket, was showing a map. "Ladies and gentlemen, this is a never to be repeated offer! You can purchase one of the two-acre lots in this riverside paradise, just ten miles away from the village, and in a park-like setting! Pay your deposit now and secure your beautiful holiday home or a place for your children to build their houses and live close by!"

His stall, too, had attracted a lot of interest from the well-to-do villagers, who were clustered around the price list.

"These prices are excellent, Mr. Hopkins," Mary heard one of the men say in approving tones. "For a riverside lot in this area, it's a steal!"

"Do we pay the deposit now?" a woman in a large, yellow hat asked, patting her purse as if she was ready to pull out her fountain pen immediately.

The next stall was attracting a poorer but hungrier set of customers, who were all eager to get their hands on Bertha's Delicious Confectionery and Cupcakes. Bertha herself, a plump woman with a broad smile, was selling scones, cupcakes, macaroons and éclairs as fast as a young woman who looked like her daughter, could unpack more of them from the big cardboard boxes at the back of the stall.

What a fascinating mix of temptations there were to choose from! No wonder this gathering was attracting visitors from miles away. Mary had never been to such a unique event. She was so interested in the variety of goods on offer, that she forgot all about being worried for Lady Beaumont's jam making success – for a moment or two, at least.

"Shall we do the maze, and then take a look at the races, and then – do you want to go on a pony ride?" she asked Hannah, her thoughts flitting back to Gilbert, who she knew liked to ride his horses around their estate. He'd told her so while they were on holiday, and ever since then, Mary had thought she'd like to learn how to ride. Just so that she could go with him one day, if she ever got the chance to visit his estate – and of course, only at a slow, gentle walk. She didn't think she'd be brave enough to go faster.

"I think that sounds like an excellent schedule," Hannah said.

But Mary couldn't resist a quick peek into the main pavilion as they passed. All the entries were already set out for the various competitions. It appeared that even though the judging was being announced later in the day, the actual assessment took place earlier.

As she walked in, enjoying the coolness of the shade after the heat of outside, she saw a disturbing sight.

Lady Beaumont was heading out of the tent, her hands clasped in front of her, her gaze fixed ahead. She looked furious, and Mary's eyes widened as she saw her march through the doorway. She seemed so preoccupied it was as if she didn't even notice Mary or Hannah.

Mary gave Hannah a concerned glance as they headed in. At the judging table, a ruddy-faced man in a black suit, with a label on his lapel that read, "Patrick Smythe: Organizer", was welcoming another man in a tweed suit. This man, with a lean build and a balding head and spectacles perched on his narrow nose, was walking slowly alongside the table where the jams were displayed.

His face was set in a sneer as he surveyed the entries.

"Well, Mr. Harold Thompson," the organizer said genially, "what an honor it is to welcome you to our event. This will be your first time judging here?"

"That's correct," the tweed-suited man replied. "Never before have I had the honor of being invited to judge locally, although I've lent my expertise to several other well known fairs and competitions. I've always felt it was due to a rather – er – prejudiced streak among certain locals," he added huffily as he surveyed the jams. "I'm a pillar of the community, but nobody appreciates that."

"I hope you find this year's entries to be of the highest quality," the organizer said.

Harold Thompson shook his head, giving the man a nasty smile. "I've felt for some years that certain jams have won on reputation rather than merit," he said. "Already, as I walk down the line, I can see that there are some jams distinctly lacking in quality. It's obvious from a mere glance that focus has been lacking. I feel there might be a shake-up this year. Some of our proud locals might find themselves knocked off their thrones."

He chuckled to himself. Mary didn't like the sound of that chuckle at all. It had a mean note to it.

A knot of fear tightened inside her as she realized what this might mean. The judge clearly had major issues with some of the competitors who were tipped to win. And what if he made sure they didn't? What if the judging ended up being unfair?

Giving Hannah a concerned glance, Mary could see that she was just as anxious.

"Looks like Lady Beaumont might have something to worry about," Hannah whispered.

"Yes," Mary whispered back. "I think so too. This judge hasn't even tasted the jam yet. He's only just looked at the jams. And already, he's saying there are issues with the quality? Really?"

"I doubt that's possible," Hannah insisted. "Lady Beaumont's jam looked flawless to me."

"I feel so badly for poor Lady Beaumont," Mary hissed back. "I think she knew immediately there was a problem with this judge. The way she walked out, that expression on her face, you could see it straight away. Now she's going to lose this competition, and it means the world to her. Her jam's all she has now that her husband is gone!"

Mary took a deep breath, trying to gather her distressed thoughts. There was nothing she could do, she told herself firmly. Most likely, Lady Beaumont had already come to terms with the situation, unfair as it was. Her angry expression had definitely indicated that. At least it wouldn't be a shock to her if she didn't win this afternoon.

Mary decided to head outside and not subject her ears to any more of this scathing and inaccurate critique of fine jams. Turning her back on the unpleasant, tweed-suited judge, she hurried outside.

There, to her surprise, she almost bumped into somebody she recognized – from a photograph in one of the newspaper clippings that she'd accidentally seen in Lady Beaumont's study. This was the jam maker who had been lauded as a huge local talent. She remembered his name was Samuel Blackwood. His looks were very distinctive – a heavily built man with a fleshy face and a head of hair that looked as if it had been cut using a pudding bowl. He was wearing a sky-blue suit and purple shoes.

Samuel Blackwood clearly had issues with the world at this moment – and everyone in his immediate vicinity.

"What do you mean you won't withdraw your entry?" he demanded loudly.

As she quickly dodged left to avoid bumping into him, Mary realized his angry words were addressed to Lady Beaumont. Samuel was standing with his hands on his bulky hips, staring at Lady Beaumont in a confrontational way.

She quickly stepped back, flattening herself against the pavilion wall, not wanting to interrupt this heated conversation.

"I entered under the competition rules," Lady Beaumont told him calmly. "As did you, Mr. Blackwood."

"Yes but – but you can see who's judging. That man's prejudiced against all of us. There's not a soul in this village he likes. He's going to mark down all our jams. All of them!"

"That might be so, but it's no reason to withdraw our entries before the judging is done. We have to be sportsmanlike," Lady Beaumont replied to Samuel, sounding annoyed by the very suggestion.

"Of course, it's a reason! It's a very good reason. We might as well make the gesture now and show him that we have no faith in his judging ability! Otherwise we'll all be humiliated when the judging is done!" Samuel seethed.

"I see no point in setting an example of bad sportsmanship," Lady Beaumont said, a note of steel in her voice. She was displeased by Samuel's bullying manner, even though it was clear to Mary that they both hated this judge equally.

Samuel sighed. "You're being ridiculous," he blustered. "I can't withdraw on my own. That's not making a gesture. It's only making a gesture if the top two or three jam makers refuse to participate. That judge needs it done to him. I can already tell you now, he's going to be making a lot of people angry, including myself. Unbearable little man!"

"I'm sorry," Lady Beaumont said firmly, "you'll have to look elsewhere for your support, Samuel. I'm not going to get involved in a public imbroglio of that nature."

Imbroglio? Mary felt elated by the sheer magnificence of that word. But Samuel didn't seem nearly as impressed by the lady's strong statement.

"Humph. Well, you'll end up the loser. If nobody's with me, then all I can say is – the judging had better be fair, or else." Turning, he marched away.

This day had started out so full of promise. Mary hadn't believed there was anything to worry about, and that Lady Beaumont's jam would certainly receive a highly commended mention, even if she didn't win.

Now, the competition seemed to be devolving into a morass of resentment, grudgery and devious agendas.

And there was only one person to blame. Seething in anger, Mary acknowledged it was all the fault of the prejudiced and unethical judge, Harold Thompson.

Why was he so hell-bent on criticizing the local jams?

A bold idea popped into Mary's head.

He had no idea who she was. If she managed to get into a conversation with him, casually – accidentally, almost, she might find out why he was so prejudiced. Mary wasn't wearing her housemaid's uniform, and she didn't look like a servant at this moment. There was no way he'd know she was working for one of the contestants.

Maybe, at close quarters, he'd prove to be a different person, and then the anxiety she felt about the results would be alleviated. Or else, she'd get an insight into his thinking, and that might help all the competitors.

Talking to the judge might be speaking out of turn, but she could only try. What could possibly go wrong?

CHAPTER FIVE

With one final, sneering glance at the jams, Harold Thompson put down the teaspoon he'd been using to prod the samples, turned on his heel, and stalked out of the tent through a side entrance. Poised for action, Mary was ready. She rushed through the tent, dodged around the tables, and followed him out.

Which way had he gone?

There he was. The man was weaving through the crowds, zigzagging left and right, and Mary immediately realized it would be difficult to find the chance to speak to him, because he seemed to know everybody. Unpopular though he clearly was, it didn't stop him from going out of his way to greet person after person.

Although when Mary thought of the word 'greet', it didn't really align with what this judge was doing. On a seemingly random basis, he was grabbing people by their arms, drawing them aside, and whispering quick words in their ears. Mary watched him do this to about four or five different people, and all she could conclude was that nobody seemed to like what he had to say.

They all reacted in different ways.

A well dressed lady with blond ringlets wrenched her arm away from his, bared her teeth at him, and stalked off, followed by his mocking laugh. A stout man, who was at a stall selling postcards, stationery and Union Jack flags, looked pale when he saw Harold heading his way. He tried to leave the stall, but tripped over the metal frame and ended up flailing in a bent-over position across the counter, while Harold muttered something in his ear.

Then, he made a bee-line for a well dressed elderly man in a top hat and tails, who was carrying a walking stick in one hand, and holding a small terrier's leash on the other. The elderly man blanched when Harold walked up to him. Then, they started having an intense argument, but in such low voices that Mary couldn't pick up what was being said.

How could one person spread so much discord, discomfort, and downright resentment? It was as if a dark cloud of conflict was following him around.

In fact, now that Mary was looking closely, she saw a number of people veering out of his path, making a conscious effort to avoid him.

She watched as a well-dressed man, walking with his wife, saw Harold coming and practically dragged the wife out of the way, disappearing at speed behind a neighboring stand. The stand was the house sales, and Harold stopped there, giving the salesman a long, considering look, and a blatant sneer. The salesman looked away, turning his back on Harold. And then, to her surprise, Mary saw that someone was tapping the unpleasant judge on the shoulder. It was a woman dressed in an old, patched gown, carrying a faded sunhat in her hand.

He spun around, saw the woman, and looked her up and down with a calculating gaze. As the woman began speaking to him in an earnest voice, Mary wished she was close enough to pick up what they were saying. It seemed like a very intense conversation, and she sensed that the woman wanted something from him.

But whatever it was, this odious jam judge was not cooperating. He shook his head, laughing in her face, and then he elbowed past her and continued his path through the crowds. Speeding up, he turned abruptly and was out of Mary's sight.

She tried to follow, but as she did, a group of elderly women flocked out of a stall selling tea and cakes. With their lively conversation, nodding gray heads, and slow-paced walks, they made it impossible for Mary to follow. There was simply no way to push through this tightly packed cluster of seniors.

She'd lost Harold without even having had the chance to speak to him. She had no idea what his opinion was on the local jams, or the jam makers, or why he held them in such contempt. Was he angry because he hadn't been asked to judge before? Or was he simply convinced that he was better and more important than anyone else in the village?

Mary didn't know, but she sensed that there were complex relationships in play. This unpopular judge had gone on the prowl. He seemed to have an agenda involving almost everyone in the village. Perhaps it was nothing more than the need to sow discord and bad blood.

Leaving angry, upset people in his wake, he'd disappeared from sight. Mary resolved to keep looking for him, but she resigned herself to the fact that she might not find him before the judging took place.

It might be better, she decided, to go back to the tent. It was going to get crowded later. At least if she was there early, she'd be in the front row when the dramatic moment came for the results to be announced.

***

"And now, we progress to the final results of our local competition, which is, of course, going to be the day's most exciting announcement. Ladies and gentlemen, as you know, this is always one of the most closely fought displays of our talent."

Mary watched nervously as, his face flushed with excitement, the organizer spoke over the microphone that had been set up in the marquee.

Compared to earlier, Mary thought, there was barely a space to be found in this enormous pavilion. It was crowded with onlookers, and a sense of breathless expectation hung in the air. The air itself carried the scent of sugar and fruit and frosting from the treats on the side tables that had been sliced and scooped and spread and, finally, judged.

At exactly four p.m., even the weather had taken a somber turn. After a day of brilliant sunshine and hot temperatures, the sky had clouded darkly over and Mary suspected it might begin raining in the next few minutes.

"I would like to ask our esteemed judge, specialist in the field of fruit growing and preserves, a valued member of our community, to step forward. Mr. Harold Thompson will be announcing his winners!"

A smattering of applause swelled in the pavilion, muting quickly as the tweed-clad Harold stepped onto the small stage.

Mary guessed that he would give what she expected to be 'the usual' – some words of praise for the entrants, and some advice for those who were up and coming in the world of jam making. There seemed to be a traditional recipe for speech making that was followed at such events, in order to make sure all the protocols were followed.

But when Harold cleared his throat, Mary quickly realized that things weren't going to go the usual way this time.

In his thin, sharp voice, Harold began.

"Well, I've seen some differing standards of entries in my time, but I have to say that this year's Oaktree Village offerings, in general, lacked quality. What have you been doing? Lazing around instead of tending your fruit trees? Drinking champagne instead of correctly boiling your preserves?"

There was a stunned silence. Mary heard it broken, after a moment, by intense whispers that seemed to come from every direction, as people took in the massive extent of this insult.

"Personally, I feel that more focus needs to be given to correct fruit production and to the classic methods of jam making. Fancy methods are simply lazy and ignorant. What happened to the rustic jams of yesteryear? Why do people mess around with them, adding things like… butter to their creations?" Disgust emanated from his voice.

As Mary glanced at the shocked faces of the contestants, who were all standing on the side of the marquee in a row, she guessed that almost everyone had used butter to improve their jam's consistency.

"I would like to discourage these ridiculously newfangled methods, particularly the use of butter. It's like cheating! My advice to all of you would be to refocus on classical perfection and work harder. In other words, our jam makers should avoid getting too big for their boots. Learn the rules before you break the rules," he admonished the competitors, a couple of whom – including Samuel Blackthorn – had now turned as red as the finest raspberry jam.

"Seeing you don't respect the correct protocols, I am going to be departing from tradition myself," he said in smug tones, "and this year, I will be awarding no highly commended certificates. None! Zero! None of you deserve one!"

Now, gasps resounded from the throng.

"I feel that one jam, and one alone, deserves a ribbon. First place this year goes to the rustic strawberry jam made by Miss Gertrude Bean, who, as you know, resides on Berrydale Farm, a few miles out of the village. Congratulations, Miss Bean. You have a fairly bright future ahead."

The shocked silence was broken by a few people clapping, and by the thump of feet as Gertrude, clearly overwhelmed by her shock result, tripped and fell as she endeavored to climb onto the stage.

With his face now puce, the organizer rushed over, helped her to her feet, and assisted her onto the stage. The plump, round-faced girl looked about seventeen, Mary realized in surprise. She looked like a relative newcomer to the world of preserves and surely couldn't have made much jam in her life. She was also crimson, and with a flash of sympathy, Mary thought that was from shame as much as from shock.

In a field of such strong contenders, a result like this was going to be badly received.

The uneasy silence as she received her gold trophy was broken only by the muttering and the shuffling of feet as people began leaving. This unpopular decision, combined with the critical words from the judge, had done more than the looming bad weather to send people home.

"I don't believe it," Hannah whispered to Mary.

With a face like thunder, Samuel Blackthorn had left the line of competitors and was joining the crowds thronging out of the tent.

Mary's stomach twisted. "Look!" she hissed, nearly knocked off her feet as a woman turned to leave and jostled her. "Look. Lady Beaumont is going up to Harold Thompson!"

"What's she going to say to him?" Hannah whispered back.

Mary watched, dry-mouthed. She had a feeling that there were going to be explosions.

But to her surprise, she was wrong. With a drawn, reserved expression, Lady Beaumont simply shook Harold's hand.

"Thank you for your judging," she said coolly, and turned away with her head high.

That prompted some scattered applause from her supporters as she marched out of the tent.

Mary's heart was hammering. She'd just witnessed an act of reckless unfairness. The question was: what was she going to do about it?

Was she, too, going to walk away? Or was she going to be the one to publicly speak up against the injustice?

As Mary's resolve surged, she heard Hannah hissing beside her. "No, Mary, no, please! I can see exactly what you're going to do and don't do it, don't you do it!"

Hannah made a futile grab for her hand, but Mary was already moving too fast for Hannah to do more than brush her fingertips. With her head whirling, knowing this was a bad idea but unable to stop herself, she pushed her way through the crowds and headed for the stage, where the organizer had now retaken the microphone and was thanking everyone for attending.

Harold Thompson hadn't left yet. With a satisfied smirk, he was preening on the stage, smoothing down his oily looking hair and adjusting his cream colored tie. Mary leaped up onto the platform and marched directly over to him.

If she waited a moment longer she would lose her nerve, and she didn't want that to happen. Drawing in a quick breath, she let him have it.

"Mr. Harold Thompson? I am only a spectator, but I would like to make it known that this judging seemed grossly unfair."

He turned to her, looking angry and taken aback at being attacked. Just like a typical bully, she thought. Before he could say a word, she continued.

"You ripped well-deserved prizes away from the most experienced jam makers, your words were insulting, and the fact you gave no highly commended ribbons shows to me that it's your palate at fault, not the quality of the jams! I've been lucky enough to taste one of them myself in the making, and it was top quality and delicious."

"You don't know a thing! You're an uneducated nobody!" Harold lashed out. But there was no stopping Mary now.

"Why should you need an education to appreciate jam? You just have to love good food to do that! And it's not the point anyway. The point is that you were asked to speak as a village expert, and you basically insulted your peers. You know what that does? It reflects badly on you, not them! You're the one who had the chance to speak well of the entrants and to applaud the pride and the hard work that all these jam makers put into their jams. You didn't do that! And I think it's small minded and – and cowardly of you!"

That was it. She'd said enough. Harold was looking ready to bite her head off, his lips actually drawn back in a snarl. The poor event organizer was now breathing so rapidly she thought he might pass out. The applause coming from the crowd was the most genuine yet, and several of the remaining competitors were also applauding and cheering her words – but Mary realized she'd gone much too far.

She had no right to fling these insults so publicly. As a housemaid and a mere visitor to the event, she should never have taken this liberty.

"Who's she?" she heard somebody of the crowd ask, as she turned away and quickly jumped off the stage, heading for the exit, where a wide-eyed Hannah was waiting.

"Mary!" Hannah gasped out the word, this time, grabbing her friend's hand tightly enough that Mary couldn't possibly pull away. "That was – well, it was wonderful and terrible all at the same time. He so deserved everything you said, but also, I'm worried about those home truths you told him. I mean, you don't want this reflecting badly on Lady Beaumont, and he's just the kind of person who could twist things that way."

Now, Mary's adrenaline was ebbing. As it slowly seeped out of her, she started seeing her actions in a different light.

"I know. I should never have done that, but somebody had to say something. It was so clear what a bad decision that was."

"If he's asked to judge again, what if it reflects badly on Lady Beaumont?" Hannah asked worriedly. At least Mary could reply to that with more confidence.

"Firstly, he couldn't hate Lady Beaumont more than he already does," she said. "Nothing I could say would make things worse. And secondly, I don't think he'll be asked to judge again. Who'd bring him back in for a second time? They had a second prize, a third prize, and three Highly Commended rosettes there on the counter, not even awarded. As if they were not deserved! It's so – so completely insulting that I can't even think about it!"

She was walking blindly through the crowds as she spoke, stomping her way along with no real idea of where she was going. Looking around, she realized she'd ended up at the bar, which was almost empty, and about to close up for the day.

Feeling in her pocket, she realized she still had two of the vouchers from their admittance this morning. Might as well put them to good use,. After all that shouting on stage, her mouth was very dry.

"Is there anything we can buy with these vouchers?" she asked the barman, who straightened up from packing bottles into a crate as he inspected them.

"You can each have a glass of champagne," he said. "There's a few spare. Normally we get quite a run on the drinks after the judging, but today, it's very strange, but everyone's going straight home."

"Maybe it's the weather?" Hannah said cynically, as Mary stepped forward, gave him the vouchers, and took two glasses of champagne, each with a cocktail umbrella and a cherry in.

She and Hannah retreated to the corner of the bar, and Mary sipped her drink.

"I'm starting to feel bad," she admitted.

Hannah rolled her eyes. "I knew you would," she said.

"It was just that it seemed so right to say those things at the time. Now I feel I should at least go and apologize."

"Wait, you want to *apologize*?" Hannah's voice quivered with nerves. "Mary, I think the best idea might be to go home. That judge is going to be mad at you, and you don't want to cause any more trouble or get into any worse fights with him."

Mary sighed. "That's a risk, I know. But I can't just let this go now. I won't let myself get into a fight with him, but I do want to offer an apology for how emotional and outspoken I was."

It had been an emotional day, she realized. She'd had a lot going on in her own head to deal with, and being so invested in the success of her employer's jam, that shock result had been the last straw.

"That's Mary Adams for you," Hannah said wryly. "I knew you were going to end up regretting that outburst and deciding you needed to make things right. Remember if you'd stayed where you were, and not spoken to him at all, like I tried to tell you to do, you wouldn't have to apologize now."

Mary sighed.

"You were right and I was wrong," she admitted. "It would have been a much better idea to stay quiet. I wish I was that person."

"I don't wish you were that person," Hannah said affectionately. "For all my warnings to you, Mary, I do admit that we need people in this world who are brave enough to speak up when they see things that are wrong."

With a final swallow, Mary finished her champagne and set the glass down.

"You wait here," she said to Hannah. "I'll go and find him, and square this up with my own conscience. Hopefully, I'll be back in ten minutes."

Checking the time, Mary glanced again at the threatening sky, she headed out of the tent. Harold might already have left. If he hadn't, then where in this emptying fairground might he be?.

Deciding that the organizer might know, she went straight back to the main marquee. Things were wrapping up fast here. The stage was being dismantled, and all the cakes and jams were being packed away into large boxes that said, "Orphanage Donation."

That was kind, Mary thought. At least all the orphans would have a wonderful treat to look forward to tonight. They'd appreciate the jams, even if the judge hadn't.

She spotted the organizer, still red-faced but looking calmer than he had when she'd been on stage. Quickly, she walked up to him, seeing that he turned to her in alarm as she approached. He flung up a defensive hand.

"Now, now, young lady!" he said in warning tones. "I don't have time for any more trouble, you understand?"

"It's alright," Mary explained. "I was wondering if you knew where Harold Thompson is? I would like to apologize for some of the things I said to him earlier."

The organizer looked surprised, as if he wasn't used to people doing things like that.

"Well, there's a tent behind this one, where we set up a table with free food and drinks for all the judges. The jam judging was the final event, and the last I saw of him, he was heading there. But please, no trouble?"

"I promise there won't be trouble," Mary reassured him.

She turned and wove her way out of the pavilion, turning in the direction he'd pointed, and spotting the small tent on the side.

As she entered the tent, Mary wondered exactly what she was going to say, and how she was going to word this apology.

She didn't want to end up criticizing him all over again, but nor did she want to retract her words entirely. It would be better to emphasize that she'd spoken in anger, and her words had been too harsh. That seemed like a sensible middle ground.

But to her annoyance, her planning was all for nothing, because she couldn't see anybody inside. There were a few armchairs set along a wall, a large table with some remnants of food and drink near the back, and a clipboard on the ground near the table.

What was a clipboard doing on the ground? Wasn't that the same clipboard that Harold himself had been carrying?

With worry flaring inside her, Mary moved forward.

And it was then, in the shadows behind the table, that she saw him.

Two shiny shoes. Two tweed clad legs. Two arms, lying limply near his head, and two staring, sightless blue eyes.

Mary gasped, an inhalation of pure horror.

Harold Thompson was lying on the trimmed grass behind the table, surrounded by the shattered fragments of the champagne bottle that had clearly been used to kill him.

CHAPTER SIX

Ten minutes ago, Mary thought numbly, it had seemed as if the summer gathering had been all but deserted. Now, crowds were thronging around as a chilly drizzle began to fall. She heard concerned voices, shouts, the occasional scream, and footsteps thudding over the grass as the news of the murder spread.

She and Hannah were sitting side by side on a bench in the organizer's office. Her first action, on seeing the dead body, had been to rush back to the main pavilion and call him. He'd stared in consternation at the corpse before telling Mary to go straight to his office and wait there.

She had detoured to the bar to tell Hannah, who'd insisted on coming with her. And now, in apprehensive silence, the two of them were waiting for the police to arrive.

"He was killed with a champagne bottle, and I'd just been drinking champagne!" Mary couldn't believe the unlucky coincidence, which she was sure would make people put two and two together and believe she was the killer.

"You were on your way to apologize," Hannah said. "You told the organizer that was what you intended to do, didn't you?"

"Yes, but the organizer didn't exactly seem to trust my temper," Mary admitted. "He was pleading with me not to cause any more trouble. It wouldn't take a lot of imagination on his part to believe that I changed my mind about apologizing, and grabbed a champagne bottle instead."

Hannah shook her head regretfully. "It's terrible luck, but Mary, you mustn't be worried. It was quite clear to me that every single one of those jam makers would have liked to murder Harold, and most probably, one of them did just that."

"The problem is that none of them criticized him to his face." Mary inwardly bemoaned her need to speak the truth as she saw it. Why had she done that? If only she'd known that somebody had been angry enough to murder Harold. She'd have done things so differently.

Too late now, and as a shadow darkened the entrance, Mary looked up apprehensively.

"Right we are. What do we have here? Is this the young lady who caused the commotion in the pavilion earlier?"

The large, solid police officer stepped forward, adjusting his helmet as he approached.

"Yes, Constable Davies. This is the lady who confronted the victim," the organizer confirmed from behind him, and Mary swallowed hard.

She needed to stand up for herself and make sure this constable had the full picture. It would be all too easy for everyone to blame a maid. And it would be more advantageous for the gathering, and the competition, too.

After all, the jam makers were angry enough about the results without being accused of murder on top of it all. And the organizer would want them back at the summer gathering next year. Right now, in this tightly knit village where she was so much of an outsider, Mary wasn't sure of anything at all except that she was going to be the most convenient person to blame.

The policeman made his way into the office. He was an exceptionally tall man, with broad shoulders, closely cropped graying hair, and a deliberate manner about him.

He folded his arms and stared down at Hannah and Mary for a few beats before speaking.

"Well, young ladies," he said. "A murder in Oaktree Village is certainly unusual. We are a peaceful place. Don't often have people killing each other in a reckless temper, as the evidence is pointing toward. Now, I believe that the woman who had the confrontation with Harold Thompson, and who then reported the body, is one and the same person. Which of you is it?"

Mary didn't like the way he phrased that. It sounded as if killing was just the middle step, nothing more than a blank to be filled in. But there was nothing she could do except reply.

"Constable, that was me."

The organizer then beckoned to Hannah, who stood up and left after giving Mary a frazzled glance. Constable Davies turned and closed the door. Then, he strode over to the desk, pulled out a chair, and sat down, gazing at Mary thoughtfully for a few moments before opening his notepad.

"Your name?"

"Mary Adams, sir. I'm working for Lady Beaumont on a temporary basis," she said.

"Temporary basis?"

"Filling in for staff on long leave." She was worried that his tone so far was suffused with suspicion. She was willing to bet that this constable had already made up his mind about her guilt.

"And why did you confront this judge, publicly, just an hour before he was murdered?" he asked.

Mary's mind raced. This constable had actually given her a new piece of information, which was that Harold's murder must have been very recent. She hadn't touched the body since it was obvious from his staring eyes and stillness that he'd been dead. A policeman would have been able to assess the time of death with greater accuracy – from the warmth of the body, she supposed.

She must have just missed the murderer! Imagine if she'd arrived when he or she was still there. There might be two bodies lying in the judges' tent now.

But she was getting ahead of herself. Dragging her thoughts back to the question at hand, Mary tried to answer it in a way that wouldn't further prove her guilt in the policeman's eyes.

"I felt that Harold's judging was very disrespectful and hurtful to the competitors. He criticized the jams of many fine jam makers, and refused to award most of the prizes because he said the jam wasn't up to scratch."

Now, a puzzled frown was creasing the constable's face. "But Oaktree jam is the best in the whole county. Everyone knows this is the leading village in terms of jam-making."

It might be premature, but Mary felt a flash of relief that the jam's reputation had spoken in her defense.

"Exactly," she continued. "Working for Lady Beaumont, I've seen the effort she put in. I could tell how angry everyone was. I guess I wanted to call the judge out on his prejudiced behavior because he was insulting and hurtful to the jam makers."

"Hmmm," the constable said. He paused. "After you said that, where did you go?"

"I went to the bar with my friend Hannah. We had a glass of... champagne."

Oh, what an incriminating word that was. If only they'd been offered some other drink by the barman, that didn't have such a direct association with this terrible crime.

"But then you went back to find Harold Thompson?" Constable Davies asked.

"Yes. I decided I should apologize for some of the stronger things I said. Just to clear the air between us, you know, because my mother said you should never let the sun go down on an argument," Mary explained.

"And you say you found him dead?"

"Yes. I didn't notice him immediately. It was only when I saw his clipboard on the grass that I looked behind the table, and there he was." Mary swallowed, hard. Death was never an easy or pleasant thing to revisit.

It seemed, though, that her words had granted her a stay of execution, temporarily at least. The constable was nodding sagely.

"It seems that this warrants further investigation," he said. "The comments that were made about the jam certainly merit a few more questions being asked. However, I must warn you that you are a strong suspect. I may need to bring you in at any time. Do not leave the village," he warned her.

With a sigh, he jotted a few final notes on his pad, and then, he got up and strode out.

Mary waited for a slow count of five, her heart pounding. She wasn't going to be arrested – yet. The unfairness of the jam judging was the only mitigating factor, but this had at least delayed the constable's decision.

She was worried, though. And as she left the office, hoping that the constable wouldn't be in sight, she saw Hannah, crouched behind a pile of two straw bales, peering at the office door.

As soon as Hannah saw Mary come out, she rushed from her temporary cover.

"Mary! I was so worried. I thought you were going to be arrested. The way the constable and that organizer were talking – it sounded as if it was a done deal."

"I think he wanted to do just that," Mary agreed, letting out a shaky breath. It was premature to feel relieved, but things could be worse right now. "The reputation of the jam was what caused him to hesitate. He was horrified to hear that the judge had criticized Oaktree jam."

"Well, that's a relief," Hannah said. "Shall we get home now? I think we need an early night, because who knows what tomorrow will bring?"

With a shiver, Mary knew it could bring bad news or an imminent arrest. In the chilly drizzle, this village green seemed like a spooky place. It was almost empty of people, and a feeling of threat hung in the air. The blustering wind was snatching at a piece of canvas, making a noise that sounded like gunshots, and which was making Mary jump.

"Let's get home," she agreed.

***

An hour later, dressed in warm, dry clothes, Mary headed down to the staff pantry with Hannah. Although she didn't really feel hungry, she knew that she needed to keep up her strength in this dire situation. And there was another reason why she was eager, and hopeful, about going down to the pantry.

She was sure word had spread, but with almost all the staff having the day off, at least there was nobody around. If Lady Beaumont had heard Mary was a suspect, she hadn't yet taken any action.

Just outside the pantry door was a table, with a roster of duties, and also a letter rack. Every day, Mary checked that letter rack with a fast-beating heart, hoping that there would be a letter from Gilbert.

And this afternoon, there was. She grabbed it from the rack, and knowing that the gesture was exaggerated, but feeling she deserved it after the day she'd had, she clasped it to her heart.

"He wrote?" Hannah confirmed with a grin.

"He did!" Suddenly, the day seemed brighter. Mary forced herself to wait before opening the letter, and instead, she helped Hannah prepare them both a light meal. A cup each of sugary tea, with creamy milk. Some of the leftover cheese and fruit from the cheese platter that Lady Beaumont had served her guests for tea, and some of the crusty bread that seemed to be a delicious staple in the kitchens of Beaumont Place.

Only when that was done, and their food was ready, did Mary open the letter.

"My dearest Mary," it began in Gilbert's neat, careful writing. *"I hope you are well, and I've been missing you terribly. I keep having dreams about us walking on the beach. If only we could go back in time to that holiday! I've been very busy down here, seeing up to five people a day, and the business is going really well. The people who planted spring seeds are already seeing a big improvement. That's helping me a lot!*

But the downside is that I have not had time to come further north and see you. How are you doing? Are you happy in your work and enjoying it there? How much longer do you have to work there before the replacement staff come back? I think it's about a week. I will try to be back before then. The next couple of days are much quieter, and if I have time, I'll take a drive. Love, Gilbert."

He said love. Mary read that word again and again. On the paper was the word she now knew to be in both their hearts. What they felt for each other was love. There was no denying it, and now the only question was to see where it would take them.

She sighed.

If only she could write a happy, upbeat letter back, describing all the excitement of the summer gathering. But no. Thanks to unfortunate events, she was going to have to be honest, spill out the harsh truth of her situation, and hope the letter reached him before Constable Davies decided to arrest her.

Mary took a mouthful of the crusty bread, tasty and light, with the sharp, dense cheese a perfect complement. Then, taking a piece of paper and a pen from the writing pad in the desk drawer that the staff were allowed to use, together with the envelopes and stamps, and then she began her reply.

"Dear Gilbert. It was wonderful to hear from you, and I am so happy your business is doing well. You deserve it after all your hard work. Which seeds are selling best?"

That was the easy part. Now for the difficult section of the letter.

Keeping it short and to the point, and trying to keep emotion firmly off the page, she described what had played out in Oaktree Village today, and how she was now a suspect, thanks to speaking out on behalf of the jam makers.

She ended it, Love, Mary.

It felt good to write that word, but she wished it could be in better circumstances.

Mary swallowed the last piece of sliced strawberry just as the cook walked in.

"Oh, dear," she said, seeing Mary. "I heard there was a bit of an incident at the summer gathering. The other maids were saying you might be arrested?" She gave Mary a nervous glance, and Mary knew, with a clench of her stomach, that working here would no longer be easy or fun. Not for the near future, anyway. People would be nervous of her. They'd think she'd killed in anger. It was strange how people were so quick to believe something like that.

"Yes, there was an incident," she said firmly. "I'm not the guilty party, but the police are investigating."

Then she shut her mouth, knowing from experience that to protest her innocence wouldn't help.

Giving her a sidelong look, the cook went over to the kettle and started making tea.

With a sigh, Mary got up.

"I'm going to post this," she whispered to Hannah. There was a postbox just a couple of hundred yards outside the manor house's gate on the outskirts of the village. If she was in time for the evening post collection, Gilbert might get her letter in the morning. That would be a comfort.

She stood up and went out, pulling up the hood of her jacket and keeping the letter firmly under the folds of it so that it didn't get wet.

As she walked, the rain and the fresh air did a good job of clearing her head after the chaos of the day. Finally, Mary felt as if she was able to plan coherently.

And she knew that she was going to have to do some research on her own, if she wanted to clear her name.

"Reason? Constable Davies seems to be a slower thinker – not to be rude, but it's the impression I got. He's worked in the village for decades, he knows all the locals, and of course he's going to suspect the outsider," she muttered to herself as she walked. "I was there at the time and saw people's reactions. I know who was there and how angry they were. And I'm part of one of the village's biggest estates. If everyone knows everyone, then I can find out what they know – with Hannah's help."

Mary reached the letterbox, her shoes squelching over the grass. She took out the letter, checked the stamp was correct, and dropped it in, sending a little prayer that it would be collected tonight and reach Gilbert in the morning. It made a slithery sound as it dropped inside, as if there were other uncollected letters waiting there.

Turning away, she found her resolve was stronger and her head was clearer.

Not only was it imperative that she investigate this herself, but she also had a strong and obvious suspect to start with.

Why had she not thought of this before?

With his anger, and his jealousy, and his abortive attempts to get the competitors to resign from the competition as one, it was clear that fellow jam maker Samuel Blackwood was by far the strongest suspect.

In fact, there was a huge likelihood that he was the killer.

CHAPTER SEVEN

"Are you sure this is where he lives?" Hannah's whispered voice came from behind Mary as they crept along the pathway that wound between the berry plants. The village was thick with mist at this early morning hour, after the drizzle last night, but when it cleared, Mary guessed it would become another perfect summer's day.

"I'm not sure! You said that the butler told you that Samuel Blackwood lived on the small farm near the village, with the green door and the three acres of blueberry and cherry orchards," Mary whispered back.

"Yes, that's what the butler said. But what if the butler is wrong? What if we're trespassing on somebody else's land?"

"Isn't there a footpath here? I'm sure I saw the sign for a footpath a mile or so back. If anybody comes out, we can just say we were going for a walk and got lost."

"As long as they don't recognize you," Hannah warned.

That was a fair comment. Mary had borrowed Hannah's woolen hat for the occasion. It was far too hot for summer, but it covered her hair completely. She'd stuffed every last butter-blond lock up into its gray, chunky depths.

They were both wearing unobtrusive clothing – Mary was wearing a pair of walking trousers, and Hannah a plaid skirt. They'd aimed to camouflage themselves as best they could. And at this early hour of five a.m., they were going to see what they could find on Samuel Blackwood.

"He'll be watching out for us," Hannah said.

"At this time? I'm sure he drowned his sorrows last night after – after the disappointment." And committing the crime, she suspected. "I'm sure he will be fast asleep. And nobody in the countryside locks their doors at night."

"We're not going in!" Hannah's whisper rose to an incredulous squeak, causing Mary to turn and frown.

"Sssh. We might need to go in. Just to see if there's any evidence."

"What evidence can we find?"

"I don't know," she said. "But I think there's more to Samuel, and his motives, than we know about. If we can find out the background, then at least we can suggest to Constable Davies that he investigates him as a strong suspect, and preferably brings him in."

"Why did I agree to this?" Hannah asked in a wobbling voice.

Mary was also questioning the wisdom of her actions. It had seemed like such a good idea – the only idea – when they'd discussed it last night and gathered information on the suspected criminal. Now, Mary had to admit, it was very scary walking right up to his house.

And here they were. The white painted walls loomed through the mist. The house looked neat and well cared for. A well tamed ivy plant climbed up a trellis between two of the windows, which had green-painted shutters, and floral curtains that were still tightly drawn.

There was the front door – bright green and shiny, with a brass knocker and a doormat that said, "Welcome."

Nerves surged inside Mary. Now they were here, snooping inside the house did seem like an extreme move. They were not welcome here. It felt like a real crime – and it was. But what option was there if they were going to gather the evidence needed to prove the real killer guilty?

"This is a very difficult situation," Mary acknowledged.

"We need to rethink this," Hannah breathed. "Can't we – can't we just check his car? Maybe there's evidence in his car, if he came home late."

"That's an excellent idea," Mary said. Checking a car was a far easier move to make, especially since a suspected killer was fast asleep inside the house. Not only was it less dangerous, but it sat better with her conscience, too. Together, they tiptoed around the house.

The garden was lush and green. The grass was overdue for a trim, and Mary guessed that the jam-making had taken up the lawn mowing time in recent days. Dewy grass brushed against the bottoms of her trouser legs, which then rustled damply against her ankles. The flower beds were gorgeous. She noticed the brilliant contrast in colors, the clever placement of rocks and hanging baskets and different levels, in passing. Clearly, Samuel was a talented gardener as well as being a jam maker – and perhaps, a killer.

But when she reached the back of the house, Mary stopped and stared in surprise.

There was a small shelter next to the house, which must contain a car, because it was the right size and shape, and also, it had tire tracks leading out of it, that were visible in the neatly raked gravel that surrounded the shelter.

"He's not here!" Mary said aloud.

"Are you sure?" Hannah looked around wildly, as if there might be a car hiding elsewhere, in those floral borders, or behind the sprouting hedge.

"He must have gone out. Early."

Mary glanced at the back door, and this time, noticed something she hadn't seen before. A large ginger cat was sitting outside the door, meowing plaintively.

Mary stared at the cat in concern, and then glanced at Hannah.

"This kitty wants to go inside," she said.

Hannah tilted her head. "There's a perfectly good kitchen window. It's open wide enough for the cat to jump in. He's just being lazy."

"He's asking us to help." Mary stepped forward. Entering a house of her own accord? She wasn't sure she'd have been able to do that easily. But helping a cat? Well, that put a different light on it.

Remembering just in time that she shouldn't leave fingerprints, wrapping her sleeve around her hand, she carefully opened the door.

The cat trotted inside and jumped onto the table, where it started eating a plate of chopped chicken.

"So you can't jump onto a windowsill, but you can jump onto a table?" Hannah asked the cat dubiously.

But thanks to this encounter, which had somehow legitimized their entrance, they were both standing inside the kitchen. And, on the counter, Mary could see a folder that looked to have been left there in a hurry, still open. The folder contained papers.

If this jam maker had been looking at this folder, so soon after a gruesome murder had occurred, perhaps they were relevant? It wouldn't hurt to look, at any rate. Perhaps he'd been putting together a compendium of evidence against this hated judge, which had pushed him to do the deed.

As if her feet were moving of their own accord, Mary found herself walking across the kitchen and staring down at that folder.

It was a folder of letters.

"I think we should have a quick look through," she said in a flustered whisper. This felt all wrong. Never had she thought she'd end up prying inside someone's personal papers after finding their kitchen door unlocked. It didn't sit well with her conscience, although she had to admit that if she'd been the super-confident Detective Sherwood who'd been brought in for the last case she'd worked on, she would have sauntered in with an overload of assurance.

But she didn't feel it was her place. This felt like what it was – an act of desperation that might get them into trouble and could well get them nowhere.

Hannah sighed. "Alright," she said. "Give me half of them, and I'll take a quick look through. If we see anything suspicious…"

"We tell the constable," Mary emphasized.

She divided the pile roughly into half, and handed Hannah the bottom half. Quickly, Mary began reading through the letters.

They were eye-opening! At any rate, her eyes were widening as she read them.

It was clear, from the replies, that Samuel Blackwood had known who the judge was going to be. The first letter proved it.

"My dear Sam, what bad luck in terms of the judge. What possessed them to use that odious Harold Thompson? He's extremely biased against you. I suggest you complain. If only you could – I don't know, kill him off, or something? Haha! Just a joke, of course! Let me know how you fare! With best regards, Lord Burnsby."

The next one was also telling.

"My dearest Samuel, you must not let the disapproving presence of a biased judge impact upon your talented crafting of the village's finest jam. You know you make the best jam in Oaktree. Don't let the childish behavior of a sad, inadequate, devious man put you off your goal. With love, Mother."

The cat had finished eating. A movement from the window sill caught Mary's attention and she whipped around to see the ginger cat climbing deftly through the window and jumping down outside.

A moment later, she realized why the cat had done that.

There was a faint, but distinctive, noise outside – the sound of an approaching motor car.

Wherever Samuel Blackthorn had been, he was coming back.

CHAPTER EIGHT

"We need to get out!" Frantically, Mary grabbed the letters from Hannah, shuffling them all into order again and replacing them in the folder, which she then put in its exact position on the counter. She didn't think that Samuel would notice it had been moved, but that wasn't the problem.

The problem was that they couldn't get out. The car was already swinging around the house and into sight.

"The front door!" Hannah whispered, grabbing her hand.

Mary rushed behind her, trying to shake off the certainty that they would be discovered. All Samuel Blackthorn had to do was walk through to the living room where they were now crouching. The sparsely, though elegantly furnished home offered few opportunities to hide. Now nestled behind a floral couch on the sky blue carpet, with Hannah beside her, Mary was trying to be as quiet as she could.

If possible, she shouldn't even breathe.

But the footsteps she now heard entering the kitchen didn't come any further. The next moment, she heard a comforting sound – the hiss of a kettle starting to boil.

He was making tea, and that gave them a chance.

"The front door?" Craning from behind the couch, she pointed in its direction.

Hannah nodded. "Perhaps we can open it and sneak out?" she mouthed.

This was going to be so risky. If the door made a noise, there was nowhere for them to go. And Samuel would be enraged.

Mary stood up, and tiptoed to the door, trying to move as quietly as that sweet, though spoiled, ginger cat had done. She reached the door and grasped the handle, forgetting about using her shirt this time.

She turned it as quietly and carefully as she could, and to her astonishment, it swung smoothly open.

Lightheaded from tension, Mary stepped outside, with Hannah behind her. She closed the door as cautiously and slowly as she'd opened it, fearing that at any moment she'd hear an enraged bellow from inside, and Samuel would wrench it right out of her hand and demand to know what they'd been doing.

But she closed the door without anyone hearing, and then, Mary led the way along the gravel pathway to the road. And then, with a huge sigh of relief, she and Hannah were walking back down the quiet country lane toward Beaumont Place.

"That," Mary said in a shaking voice, "was one of the most terrifying experiences I've ever had. We shouldn't have been in there and prying around, and I feel very bad for bringing you with me." She turned apologetically to Hannah.

Hannah stared at her wide-eyed. "What are you talking about? I enjoyed that! It was a huge thrill."

"What?" Mary felt shocked by this admission.

"I felt like a real detective, like that one you were talking about after the last case."

"Yes," Mary replied, feeling a little better now. "I was thinking about Detective Sherwood, too, in there."

"So, did you find anything from those letters?" Hannah asked.

Mary sighed. "You know, Samuel was definitely jealous and angry about that judge. He knew Harold was going to be judging, and he was trying to figure out what to do. One of his friends jokingly suggested killing the judge."

Hannah frowned. "Well, the problem with this logic is that it would have made much more sense for Samuel to have killed Harold before the competition. Then they would have had to have found another judge, wouldn't they?"

"Yes," Mary said. "It would have made more sense to do that, but I don't know if sense was even part of the equation here. This seemed to be a very emotional action. Someone was angry with that judge."

"Maybe Samuel was hopeful right until the end, and only when he realized the judge was going to punish all the local jam makers, was he angry enough to do what he did."

"I think that could have been what happened," Mary said. "So he's still not ruled out. But what about your letters?"

Turning to Hannah, Mary noticed that she had a knowing expression on her face, as if that was a question she'd been waiting for Mary to ask.

"Did you find something?" Mary was now even more curious.

Hannah shrugged. "I might have done," she said, as they turned through the ornate gateway of Beaumont Place, and headed up the long driveway.

"What?" Mary asked. "Come on, tell me! What did you find?"

Hannah leaned closer to her. "Did you ever hear of the name Clara Thompson?"

The name Thompson got Mary's eyes widening.

"She must be a relation to the judge, I'm guessing?" she asked.

Hannah nodded. "From the letter I read, it seems that Clara Thompson is the estranged daughter of the judge. She hated her father. She had no love for him at all and thought his behavior was despicable. From what she wrote, he always used to put people down, and went out of his way to ensure they were disappointed and humiliated. I think he basically bullied, or somehow coerced, the organizer into using him as the judge, and it looks like it was Clara herself who told Samuel that her father was going to be the judge. So she leaked the news."

Puzzled, Mary glanced at Hannah as they headed around the house, toward the kitchen door. It was six-thirty a.m., and she was relieved that they were back in time to start their working day.

But what Hannah had said didn't make sense.

"Why would Clara Thompson be telling Samuel Blackwood all of this?" Mary asked her friend, still sensing that there was more she hadn't told.

Hannah paused dramatically with her hand on the door handle.

"Because, from what I read, it seems like Clara and Samuel were having an affair," she revealed. "She seems to adore Samuel and was hoping that he'd win the competition regardless."

Mary stared at her, shocked.

"But that means…"

"Exactly," Hannah said. "It means that not only did Samuel have a strong motive for killing the judge in anger – but his own daughter did, too."

***

Mary's mind was buzzing with ideas as she began her daily tasks. She'd never dreamed that their illegitimate foray into Samuel's house would reveal so much shocking information. Samuel had been having an affair with the judge's estranged daughter?

Did they work in tandem? Had both of them committed this crime? Had Clara done it in a blaze of protective anger, enraged on her lover's behalf?

Or had Samuel done it, furious about the insults to his jam?

With the dustpan and brush in her hand, she walked into the formal drawing room to sweep the carpets, and heard a frightened yell.

One of the other housemaids was standing on a ladder. She'd been taking down one of the curtains for cleaning, but when she saw Mary come in, she nearly fell off the ladder.

"Oh, it's – it's you! You're working today?" Her voice was incredulous. "Shouldn't you be in prison?"

Mary sighed. "I'm not guilty. It wasn't me who killed that judge." She tried to lower her defenses, which had automatically soared sky-high. Being defensive wasn't helpful. With an effort, she tried to adopt a more approachable tone, and even managed a smile.

"You know me. We've worked together for more than six weeks! I hope you wouldn't think I was a killer."

"Well, I suppose not."

Reluctantly, the other maid climbed back up the ladder.

"The reason I even found the body was that I was looking for him to apologize for the strong words," Mary admitted.

Now, the other maid glanced at her with a trace of sympathy on her wide, pleasant face.

"And haven't we all been in that predicament? There have been many times I've wanted to speak my mind, I must admit."

"It felt – well, it felt very scary to stand up and criticize him in that way," Mary said. "It's one thing to think about doing it, but quite another to do it. I thought he deserved it, though, because he was so unfair. But then, of course, I had regrets. Unfortunately, it was too late, and somebody had killed him by the time I got there."

"Oh." The housemaid nodded understandingly. "Yes, that makes sense. I think I'd apologize too, if I was ever brave enough to do such a thing. But it sounds as if he was a nasty piece of work. Someone else must have been angry enough to – to do that final thing."

"Tell me," Mary said, "changing the subject, I have been wanting to speak to Clara, his daughter. I don't know her – do you?"

"Clara Thompson? Yes, I know she lives in the village."

"Would you know where she stays? After – after what happened, I thought it might be polite for me to get in touch with her, and perhaps send some flowers."

The housemaid frowned, clearly wondering why Mary was going to such trouble for somebody she'd never met, but she guessed her tone was innocent enough, because the woman replied without undue suspicion in her tone.

"Let me think. I've sometimes taken produce to her house. We supply a lot of the villagers with berries, vegetables and the like." She unhooked a few more folds of the curtain in thoughtful silence. "She lives near the church," she said. "Next door to it, I think. She has a house with a slate roof that needs repair. I know every time I walk past it and leave her produce on the front step, that roof bothers me." She made a wry face.

"That's very helpful," Mary said. Finally, she felt this investigation was getting somewhere. As she headed over to the rug, to begin her brushing, she felt a sense of expectancy. Motives were being uncovered, and allegiances exposed. If this continued, then she was sure that in a short time, she'd be able to find the killer himself – or herself.

With her brushing done, she headed back to the kitchen, and as she was hanging up the dustpan and brush again, she heard the words she knew could give her an opportunity.

"We've got a pint of cream here!" the cook was calling out. "A pint of cream that we need to send down to the church for their service later. Anyone willing to take it?"

The church? The same church that was next door to Clara Thompson's house? Mary couldn't volunteer quickly enough, even though she made sure to sound casual and not too eager.

"I've just finished brushing the carpets. I can go," she said. But she spoke at exactly the same time as the assistant cook.

The cook, with hands on her hips, stared from one of them to the other, as if mulling the decision over in her mind. And then, with a nod, she clearly decided that since Mary had a cloud over her reputation, she was better outside the manor house than inside.

"You go, Mary Adams," she said. "But walk fast. They'll need to get this cream in the refrigerator before it turns sour."

"I'll walk as fast as I can," Mary promised, feeling thrilled by the opportunity that she'd been able to create.

She'd go as fast as she could – but that didn't mean she would come back equally fast.

Once that cream had been handed over, she was going to take an important detour. It might just lead her to the killer's house.

CHAPTER NINE

Leaving the kitchen, with the cream in a large steel jug covered by a cloth, Mary realized with a pang that she shouldn't go to Clara's house empty handed. After such a tragedy, even an estranged daughter would surely need some token of comfort?

As fast as she could, conscious of that cream getting warmer by the minute, Mary sped to her basement room and dug in the pockets of the skirt she'd worn at the gathering.

Thank goodness. There were two shillings that she hadn't spent at the fair. She could use them at the village shop and buy a little gift to take with her to Clara. That would be the kind thing to do. After all, Clara was still only a suspected killer, but she was definitely a bereaved daughter.

Knowing this was going to be nerve-racking and likely to result in an emotional confrontation no matter what happened, Mary headed out.

It was an easy walk from the manor house to the church, but she was surprised by how busy the church was. It took her a moment to realize that since the gathering had been on Saturday, today was Sunday, and all the villagers and parishioners were coming in to attend service.

She'd become so used to the musical sound of the church bells ringing through the valley that she barely noticed them anymore. Now, close up, the clear sound of the bells resonated with her, making her glance around to appreciate the idyllic beauty of the village, with its thatched stone cottages and glorious gardens. The surrounding farmlands were lush and productive, farms that had provided for the locals even during the war's hardship. And the day was perfect now that the mist had cleared, and the sky was filled with fluffy clouds that seemed to enhance the blue in between.

Now, where in this quaint churchyard would the cream be needed?

Mary headed in the side entrance, automatically keeping her head turned away from the incoming streams of people, because in a village this small, there was going to be a sizeable overlap between gathering attendants, and church attendants. It was better for her to stay unnoticed and out of sight.

Seeing a sign for the offices, she headed that way, and arrived at a paved courtyard behind the church, with a small office opposite. Under a covered overhang, two trestle tables had been set out, covered by white cloths, and with probably a hundred cups and saucers set out.

A woman wearing a white apron over her smart church clothes was adding teaspoons to each saucer with a silvery jangling of steel.

"Ah," she said, peering from under her ginger fringe as she saw Mary arrive. "The cream! How kind of you"

And then, to Mary's dismay, her gaze sharpened.

"Wait a minute," she said as she took the cream from Mary, the jug wobbling ever so slightly as she made the connection. "You're the – the woman from the manor that everyone's been talking about. Aren't you?"

"I was the one who discovered the poor judge's body, yes," Mary said, deciding that deflecting her attention would be the best strategy. "And I'm very upset by all of it, especially having been falsely accused. Can you imagine how difficult that is?"

"Falsely…?" The woman stared at Mary for a moment, clearly thinking hard. "Oh. I see! Goodness!"

"It's very upsetting," Mary said. Wondering if she might start to confirm people's whereabouts at the time, she asked the woman, "Were you there?"

"Why yes," she said. "I was there, right in that marquee, when you stood up on stage and gave that man a piece of your mind." In a lower voice, she added, "I must say, part of me was cheering until I realized the – the awful consequences."

Mary stepped closer. In a low voice, she said, "I saw one of the jam makers walk out at an early stage, before I even said those words. His name was Samuel Blackthorn."

"Ah, yes!" The woman smiled. "Blackthorn's Berry Preserves and Fine Marmalade. They're a legend! If you ask me, he should have won!"

"Did you notice which direction he went in?" Mary asked.

Cradling the cream jug in her hands, she frowned. "Well, he didn't go in any direction."

"What do you mean by that?" Mary asked.

"He immediately left the gathering," the other woman said.

Shock resounded through Mary, and she had to fight to keep a neutral expression. Was this information correct?

"How do you know that?"

"Well, it's because of his other stall, you know. Samuel runs a very famous jam and preserves stall at Whitelake, the bigger town twenty miles north of here. He likes to run the stall himself, and I've been there many a Saturday to buy from him. But he has a rule that he's there at closing up time."

"And closing up time is?" Mary asked.

"Five p.m.," she said. "He's usually there half an hour before, to make sure the accounts all tally up, and to pack the remaining jam, so that none goes missing."

Mary blinked. "You sound as if you know this very well," she said.

"Yes, it's coincidental. We were in Whitelake just a few weeks ago, buying jam at four-thirty p.m., and he rushed in as if he'd been told about a fire. He apologized for startling us, and explained. He can be quite charming, you know, once you get past his abrupt manner."

"That's really interesting," Mary said, frantically doing mental arithmetic. But the numbers were giving no room for leeway. It would have taken at least half an hour to drive along those narrow, winding country roads, and that meant that Samuel Blackthorn had left in such a hurry after the judging because he wanted to be at his other stall before it closed.

He could not have been in two places at once. Therefore, he had not been in the judges' tent, killing Harold Thompson. Through a lucky coincidence, and some bold questioning, Mary had managed to confirm an alibi and rule out a very strong suspect.

That was disappointing. But Mary thanked the tea server in a friendly way, and even made a few remarks about the lovely weather before she left. It was vitally important when you were an amateur sleuth, not to arouse suspicion. She'd learned that the hard way.

Surprising as this bombshell was, she needed to look on the positive side. Chasing any further after Samuel Blackthorn was pointless, and now she knew she didn't have to waste her time on it.

It did not mean that Clara was innocent, and she was still a strong suspect.

Heading purposefully toward the general store, Mary racked her brains for an appropriate gift to bring along, to justify her presence on this suspect's doorstep.

Her indecision was only worsened when she walked through the doors. This store was most definitely focused on the basics. She couldn't exactly take a toothbrush with her, as a gift. It wouldn't strike the right note. Nor would a block of butter go down the way she wanted it to.

Eventually, feeling panicked because time was ticking by and the cook expected her back, she discovered a shelf with some good quality skin lotion. The scent, according to the label, was lily of the valley. It wasn't as good as bringing along a bunch of lilies, but it would have to do.

She didn't even know if Clara would be at home. She might be at church, like most of the rest of the village.

But, as she headed along toward the small house, looking out for the fault on the slate roof just to confirm to herself she was in the right place, she saw something even worse.

It took her a moment to recognize the tall man striding toward her, and that was one moment too long.

For the Sunday service, Constable Davies had removed his helmet – taking away the characteristic that made him easy to identify from a distance.

Without it, he was still tall, but looked more ordinary and less intimidating now that he was clad in a light, pale gray suit, with a lemon colored tie, fastened a little too tightly around his thick neck.

He must have been looking out for her, because instantly, his gaze sharpened.

"Miss Adams!" he called.

"Constable Davies?" Stopping in her tracks, she waited, feeling nervous but trying to appear innocent as he made a beeline for her.

"I was looking for you. I was at the manor house just half an hour ago, and after a search, Lady Beaumont informed me you were nowhere to be seen." Both his tone and his expression were deeply suspicious.

"I was asked to run an errand," Mary said. "I've just delivered a jug of cream to the church. I believe they need it for the after-service tea."

"But why didn't you tell Lady Beaumont where you were? Did I not inform you that you were supposed to be available at all times?"

"I am truly sorry," Mary said. "I didn't realize I had to inform the lady herself. The cook was the one who ordered me to do the delivery."

"Oh. I see." Now his anger had deflated, as if he'd puffed himself up ready for a big accusation which had never materialized. It seemed as if her reason for leaving the manor had placated him. And luckily, he hadn't realized that she'd been investigating.

But then, he frowned again.

"Why are you headed this way? This road goes to the north side of the village. Why aren't you going straight back the way you came?"

"Oh, no real reason," she said, her brain racing. "It's just that the road is busy with the church service, and I thought it would be nicer to walk back through the park."

She indicated up the road, toward the stretch of greenery formed the start of the local park. The park followed the course of a stream that meandered through Oaktree Village. The stream was pretty, with wildflowers and weeping willows growing alongside, and a paved walking trail near the road.

"Ah, the park." Briefly, a warm expression crossed the constable's face, as if that park held happy memories for him. Mary wondered if he had a dog that he walked there. Or maybe he'd proposed to his beloved under one of those weeping willows.

The sharp clearing of his throat brought her attention back to him.

"Miss Adams, these are minor details. There is a more important reason I've been looking for you."

"What's that?" she asked. She didn't like his tone of voice at all.

"I was urgently seeking you because a key witness, who was in the pavilion during the jam judging, has said that they saw you leaving shortly after Harold Thompson walked out, and that you were brandishing an empty champagne bottle in your hand."

CHAPTER TEN

As the constable unleashed this bombshell, Mary recoiled in shock.

"That's a complete lie!" she blurted out. "Who told you that?"

Why, oh why was the constable even entertaining this person's version? Was it that this person was a trusted member of the community and therefore above suspicion?

Was someone – perhaps even the killer – deliberately trying to frame Mary, or was this just idle gossip with a large dash of imagination thrown in?

She had no idea, but it was going to land her in terrible trouble.

The constable folded his arms. "I cannot reveal my source. It was told to me in confidence."

"Why would you believe it over what I told you? Has anyone else apart from this source confirmed it?" Mary challenged him.

He looked surprised by her aggressive response.

"There's no need to get upset," he said.

"There's every need!" Mary retorted. "My future is at stake here! I don't want to be wrongfully arrested!"

Constable Davies sighed. "What I have here, now, are two conflicting versions. You claim this witness is not telling the truth. But the witness's account contradicts yours. You'll understand why I'm concerned about this now." His voice was grim. "Everywhere I go in this village, I'm seeing how worried the local people are. I can't walk out of my house without somebody asking me when an arrest is going to be made. With a crime of this magnitude, delays reflect badly on the police. People will rightly lose confidence in the local constabulary."

Mary felt despair settling into her heart. This constable's attitude was set on steel girders, and there seemed to be no derailing it.

"Won't they lose even more confidence if you arrest an innocent person?" she pleaded.

"That is the question I'm asking myself," he replied. "I am trying to be as fair as possible by investigating this thoroughly before bringing you in. So far, though, there's no evidence pointing to anyone but you."

"Have you questioned all the jam makers who entered the competition?" she asked.

"Are you telling me how to do my job?" Now, he was the one sounding angry and offended.

Much as Mary wanted him to do his job and didn't see why she shouldn't remind him of things he might have missed, she also didn't want to make him so angry that he arrested her on the spot.

Better to remind him, politely but firmly, what her movements had been.

"As soon as I'd had words with Harold Thompson, I left the pavilion together with my friend, Hannah," Mary said. "I didn't pick up any empty bottles on the way out. I already felt bad about having had my say, and I needed to get away to calm down and think about what I should do. Hannah was with me the whole time. She can confirm I wasn't carrying anything except for two meal vouchers and a handful of spare change."

"Hannah is your close friend, and she's not an unbiased witness. Besides, you told me you went to find the judge alone."

"Well, yes. Hannah and I went out of the pavilion together, and then I left her in the bar."

"Now your story is changing." He waggled a warning finger at her.

"She stayed in the bar. I went to find the judge, detouring back to the pavilion to ask where he would be. The organizer can confirm I was not carrying an empty bottle!" Mary pleaded.

"The organizer cannot accurately recall if you were carrying anything. He chose not to answer that question," Constable Davies said. "One of the other women in the tent with him said you looked angry. Did you go to find Mr. Thompson and finish what you started?" Constable Davies asked, his brow wrinkling.

Did he think he could trap her into saying 'yes' by mistake? Well, she wasn't going to do that.

"Like I said, I went to apologize."

All she could do was stick to her story. And the constable gave a disappointed shrug, as if he'd hoped that she might break under the pressure.

"They're testing the pieces of the champagne bottle for fingerprints," he said. "If any are discovered, we will bring you in immediately. Do not, and I mean do not, leave this village." He wagged his finger one more time and then turned away, heading briskly down the road as the church bells rang out again.

He wasn't going to arrest her yet, but he wanted to, badly. She was distressed that he was so ready to believe gossip and hearsay, but Mary could see he didn't have enough hard evidence. Arresting her and then being unable to press charges successfully would not reflect well on him, so he was gathering more information as fast as he could.

That meant she, in turn, had to gather information even faster, especially since there was a risk that someone was deliberately trying to frame her.

Mary walked on, heading for the park, and she didn't look back until she had rounded the corner.

Then, she stood for a minute, counting slowly to ten.

By now, the constable should be in church. The bells had stopped ringing and that must mean the service was underway. Church would last for an hour, and so she had an hour to find and question Clara without Constable Davies seeing her.

As fast as she could, she headed back the way she'd come, this time heading to that house next door to the church. Checking it, she confirmed there was a gap in the slate roof. In fact, the gap was so noticeable that if it rained, Mary was sure that the house owner would have to place a bucket under that part of the ceiling.

And now, it was time to go in and confront that house owner.

Walking briskly up to the front door, with her impromptu gift in her hand, Mary knocked and waited.

For a few moments, she heard nothing, and she was starting to think that Clara Thompson must be at church. But then, hurried footsteps approached, and the door was wrenched open.

The woman who stared at her was in her late twenties, with bright blue eyes and russet-brown waves, and an irritated expression on her otherwise attractive, freckled face.

She was wearing gardening gloves, and must have been out back, tending to her flowers.

"Yes?" she said, in a brisk, abrupt tone. "What is it? I'm very busy now."

"I'm sorry to interrupt your gardening. I brought you this and hoped we could speak for a minute," Mary said, handing over the lotion.

Clara's nose wrinkled. "But why are you giving me this? Who even are you?"

Clara didn't look upset. She hadn't been crying. That was interesting. It told Mary something, although she wasn't sure what.

56

"My name is Mary Adams. I was at the gathering when – when the terrible incident involving your father happened. I wanted to speak to you and thought this little gift might be comforting."

Clara didn't look like she needed comfort. But then, an expression of sadness crossed her face.

"I'm sorry for what happened to my father," she said. "Yes, we hadn't spoken for years, but you're right. The fact he was killed that way is very distressing. I haven't let myself think about it much."

She took the lotion in a gardening-gloved hand and set it on the small wooden table in the entrance hall.

Now, Mary was wondering if that show of regret was real or fake. Had it been too little, too late? Was Clara realizing that she should show some sadness or it would be suspicious?

"Why had you not spoken for years?" Mary asked.

"Well," she said, "we were never really close. I was always closer to my mother, who unfortunately divorced him a couple of years ago, and moved to Sunderland. When I was in my late teens, I rebelled against his authority, and we never made up."

"And you stayed in the village, despite not speaking to him?" Mary pressed.

"Well, yes. I work in the local bakery, so why wouldn't I live here? I don't know why you feel the need to ask all this."

"Were you at the summer gathering?" Mary asked. She had the feeling that she was treading on thin ice. Clara was getting defensive.

"What business is it of yours?" She paused. "I might have gone there for a while, yes."

"I just wondered if you'd had a – a chance to speak with your father while you were there?" Mary said.

"I don't speak to my father, and I don't see why you're standing here on my doorstep, asking questions like this."

"I'm very disturbed by what happened," Mary said, trying her best to explain herself. "I was trying to piece together the circumstances."

Sighing, as if she was getting tired of explaining this, Clara said, "Like I told you, I did my best to avoid him. I'm sure that my father was doing his usual thing there, going around and talking to all the –" She closed her mouth.

"Talking to all the what?" Mary felt she was on the verge of a breakthrough. If only Clara had said a word or two more. She'd stopped at just the wrong time before Mary was able to make the connection she needed to.

And Clara wasn't saying more. Now, she glowered at Mary.

"I appreciate the gift, but I don't think you're here just to be kind. I think you're here because you want information, and you're keeping me from my gardening. I'm sick of talking about this. That police detective was pestering me yesterday evening, and now, you're doing the same this morning? Enough, already." She rubbed her gardening gloves together decisively.

So, Constable Davies had been questioning her, too? That was surprising. Mary didn't think the constable had bothered speaking to any of the locals. At least now she knew he'd spoken to one.

The problem was that if he'd suspected Clara, he had presumably cleared her. Perhaps she'd had an alibi.

"My sympathies again, and enjoy your Sunday," Mary said, recognizing that there was nothing more she could learn here. She couldn't rule Clara out altogether as a suspect, and more seriously, she knew that the judge's daughter possessed information about her father that she wasn't telling.

This had been a frustrating and incomplete discussion, she thought, as the door slammed behind Clara. But there was no such thing as a wasted interview. She had learned a few things.

So far, the jam judging, and the disappointment of the competitors, had been at the forefront of her mind. Now, she was wondering if she needed to widen her thinking.

Whatever Clara had nearly said, it had seemed important. It reminded Mary that Harold Thompson had interacted with many people in the village, while he'd been at the gathering. She didn't yet know why, but she remembered how he'd woven his way through the crowds, with nasty words for all.

Outside of being a jam judge, it seemed as if Harold Thompson had been an all-round unpleasant character. There might be other people who wanted to kill him. Someone could have taken the opportunity at the summer gathering, guessing that with so many people around, there would be safety in numbers.

How could she find out more about Harold's activities in the village? It would be a challenge, seeing nobody so far seemed willing to talk, and there was a big risk that somebody in this closely knit community would report back on her questioning to Constable Davies.

The thought weighed on Mary's mind as she hurried back along the scenic trail that led through the park. Whatever research she decided on, it would have to wait until later. Now, she needed to get back to work because she'd already spent far too much time in town.

But as Mary approached Beaumont House, she saw a car waiting at the top of the driveway, outside the mansion's front door, its engine still idling.

She recognized it, and her heart sped up as she broke into a run.

The new arrival was Gilbert.

CHAPTER ELEVEN

Gilbert must have read her letter!

Sprinting up the tree-line driveway toward his car, her heart soaring, Mary realized he must have read it early this morning, seen that there was a crisis, and driven straight here.

Climbing out of the car as she approached, he turned to her, with his face lighting up in a way that told her he was just as delighted to see her, as she was to see him. That was a relief, given the trouble she'd told him about.

Mary flew into Gilbert's arms, hugging him hard, feeling the warmth of his hands on her back, and the murmur of his voice.

"Mary, it's so good to see you again. It's felt like far too long since we were together. Far too long."

"I've missed you terribly," she admitted.

Finally, they moved out of the embrace, and Mary smiled up at him, seeing her joyful expression reflected in his eyes.

Then, a glimmer of movement at one of the mansion's upstairs windows caught her eye, and she glanced up.

Had that been Lady Beaumont? Or her son?

One of the two, she thought. The Beaumonts were watching. Neither Lady Beaumont nor Maxwell would be pleased to see their housemaid standing outside the front door of their stately home as if she owned it, hugging a guest who was her personal friend.

Especially since that housemaid was now a murder suspect.

She didn't know how the Beaumonts felt about that. They hadn't said anything so far. Either Lady Beaumont was biding her time to confront Mary, or else she was reserving judgment until the police had investigated. Either way, Mary needed to keep her head down and not draw attention to herself the way she was doing now.

As the reality of her situation came crashing back down, Gilbert stepped away, frowning as he saw her face change. Now, worry was in his eyes, too.

"I'm in a spot of trouble," she admitted.

"Your letter said so," Gilbert agreed. "It sounds very unfair."

"I need to talk to you about it – but I can't now. I'm on duty," Mary explained, and Gilbert nodded. She felt terrible. He'd dropped everything and rushed here to help her, and she couldn't even take the time to speak to him properly.

But work was work, and responsibilities were responsibilities, and she couldn't shirk them, frustrating as it was.

"When do you finish?" he asked.

"Luckily, today's my early day. I finish at five p.m.," she said.

"Early day?" His eyebrows rose.

It was a fair enough question, since she'd started work at seven-thirty. Housemaids never worked short days.

"Late would be six-thirty or seven p.m.," she acknowledged wryly.

"Well, at five p.m., I'll come back here, and I'll take you to dinner at the local restaurant," he said.

Mary felt her cheeks flush with happiness. The excitement of going on a dinner date would make the day fly by. She was looking forward to it. The local village restaurant seemed to be famous. At any rate, on the nights she'd headed out to the village for a walk, or to do some shopping, Mary had seen cars parked for hundreds of yards down the road, and delicious smells emanating from out of the open doors.

"I look forward to it," she said.

She felt much more hopeful now. Over dinner tonight, she could tell Gilbert about the situation in detail. Hopefully, he would have some fresh ideas about how to proceed, and they might point her in the direction of the killer.

***

Mary dug her fork into another piece of fish. Tender, with a hint of lemon, and perfectly grilled. The small dish of fluffy rice, flavored with saffron, and the tender chunks of steamed broccoli and carrots, completed the dish to perfection, and she couldn't get enough of the rich, tangy lemon butter sauce that they'd brought on the side.

Putting down her fork, Mary lifted her glass and took a swallow of the white wine she'd ordered. Cool, crisp and dry, it was the perfect partner to her meal.

This tasty dinner, and Gilbert's company, had soothed her jangled nerves. Sitting at a corner table of the luxurious restaurant, it felt as if she'd been transported to a different and better world, briefly leaving the stresses of life behind.

It hadn't lasted, though. In the last few minutes, as she told Gilbert about her situation, the stresses had descended again.

"So you see," she said, "there are no real suspects apart from me. If Clara was a suspect, she's been cleared by Constable Davies. The problem is that I haven't had a chance to find out anything else about Harold Thompson. Nobody seems willing to speak. I'm sure there's more to be found, though."

Gilbert shook his head. "I was so worried when I got your letter. It's such a difficult situation, but I guess this is what happens in a small village. The locals band together, and the stranger is suspected. It might also be difficult to get information for that reason," he said.

"You mean, the locals closing ranks?" she asked.

He nodded, looking grim. "Problem is, in a small town, everyone knows everyone else's secrets. That can lead to a code of loyalty even when people dislike each other. You'll have to crack that – and without being discovered? Is it even possible?" he asked in a worried voice.

"That, I don't know," she said.

The hum of voices all around them was soothing. Sitting with her back to the room, Mary felt safe in her anonymity here. The restaurant was full, and the ironic thing was that this murder was probably being discussed at every single table!

If only she could be a fly on the wall – not that she saw any flies in this immaculate restaurant, with its crisp white tablecloths and subdued gold lighting.

"I must go to the bathroom," she said, putting her fork down as she excused herself. Maybe this would give her an opportunity to overhear something.

She turned away from the table, walking slowly, keeping her ears open for any mention of the word "Harold", or the word "murder" from the tables she passed.

Or even, come to that, the word "Mary".

But the conversation was at such a low level it was difficult to pick up any voices as she passed. No doubt, everyone was lowering their voices while discussing this terrible deed.

Heading into the bathroom, which had fresh flowers on the counter and lavender soap at the basin, she headed into one of the two stalls, and closed the door. It had been a good idea to try to overhear the conversation as she'd passed, but it hadn't worked.

But as Mary was about to open the door and head back to Gilbert, she heard voices approaching.

Two women entered the bathroom, both in the throes of a conversation that had clearly been going for a while.

"Isn't it the most shocking thing, Gladys?" the first woman said. Although Mary couldn't see her, she imagined her, from her voice, as plump and pleasant looking, with graying hair.

"My dear Edwina, it's simply beyond the pale," her friend replied – a sharper voice that Mary associated with a taller, leaner, more domineering looking personality.

"Of course, many people would have had a reason to want him... *murdered.*" at that stage, Gladys's voice dropped to a mutter and Mary stepped forward, with her ear against the door.

"I always felt that one person in particular resented him," Edwina replied.

"Oh, yes. I know who you mean. The village champion, of course!" Gladys's voice rose again, and Mary's eyes widened. This just circled back again, all the way to the jam competition – and disturbingly close to home.

"I was waiting for her to take him on," Edwina said. "I was sure she was going to say something, or do something, that would put him in his place."

"That politeness was very surprising. Although, maybe she'd briefed her maid to speak out on her behalf!"

Mary clapped a hand over her mouth, hoping neither Gladys nor Edwina had heard her audible gasp. It seemed the whole village believed she was doing things she hadn't ever thought of.

"Do you think so? I thought the maid spoke her own mind," Edwina whispered, as Mary nodded supportively. "However, I definitely thought, when I heard he was murdered, that she'd put her plans in place."

"She's a very clever woman," Gladys agreed, with a mixture of fear and admiration in her voice. "At least she knows who *won't* be judging that competition again next year."

The bathroom door opened and closed, and their voices faded away as they left.

After a pause, to let them get away so they wouldn't know she'd overheard them, Mary opened the door and scurried out, breathless and shocked by what she'd learned.

There had been long term resentment between Lady Beaumont and Harold Thompson. She'd known that, of course, and seen it in the lady's demeanor. She hadn't known that feud was so serious, and she hadn't guessed that other people in the village thought that Lady Beaumont would be capable of such a crime.

The champion jam maker of Oaktree Village might have been safeguarding her future interests, hiding her hatred for the judge behind a sportsmanlike front, while making absolutely sure he wouldn't do it again.

Her own employer?

Returning to the table, Mary felt breathless with surprise. Her investigation had taken her all over the village, but now it was becoming clear that the strongest suspect might well be within the walls of Beaumont Place itself.

"I overheard an interesting conversation in the bathroom," she told Gilbert.

"Really?" His eyebrows rose. "Does this mean you're going to... pursue some inquiries?"

She knew she had to be honest with Gilbert. After all, she was in love with him, and she couldn't keep a secret from the man she loved.

"I have to," she admitted. "It's a race against time. If the constable doesn't find another suspect, there's going to be massive pressure on him to make an arrest. And as we agreed, it's because of this being such a tight-knit community, that he's not trying very hard to find anyone else."

"So, who is this person?" Gilbert asked.

Now, Mary shook her head. There were some things she wasn't ready to tell. Not until she had more information. And in this restaurant, she didn't even dare whisper the name aloud.

"I'll know more tomorrow," she replied.

Gilbert looked worried. "I wish I could be here to help you," he said. "But I have to leave before dawn tomorrow for an appointment at a farm near Birmingham. I have appointments the whole of tomorrow, right up until late. But the following morning, I'll come straight back. From then on, if you need help, I'm ready to give it."

Reaching across the table, he took her hand in his, and Mary felt herself melt at the warmth of his touch.

Gilbert was on her side. He was ready to help solve this crime, and that meant the world to her.

"With any luck," she admitted, "the killer will be caught by the time you get back. But let's see what plays out later."

He quirked an eyebrow. "This is sounding very mysterious."

"I wish I could say more," Mary said.

"As long as it's not dangerous?" Concern darkened his tone as he signaled for the bill.

"I hope not," she replied.

It was all the reassurance she could give him. As they stood up and headed out of the restaurant to Gilbert's car, Mary reminded herself that investigating a killer was never safe.

If she moved fast, she hoped she could get the evidence she needed before the killer moved against her again.

The car ride through the village took just a couple of minutes. The late evening light was starting to fade as the Bentley swung through the estate gates and headed up the driveway.

After a lingering goodnight kiss, and a promise that they would see each other the day after tomorrow, Mary climbed out of Gilbert's car. She hurried around the house, using the servant's kitchen entrance to make her way inside, and he drove off, heading to wherever he was staying tonight, before his early morning start.

Standing in the kitchen, Mary wondered how to approach this. She needed to get to grips with this possibility urgently.

"Maybe Lady Beaumont herself will let something slip?" she muttered to herself. In the past, there had been a few times where Mary had confronted the killer and provoked him, or her, into an angry outburst that had ended up confirming their guilt.

Doing that again might be the best solution.

She knew that confronting her employer after hours might be construed as rude, and that was an advantage right now. She wanted Lady Beaumont to think she was being rude, because in a fit of temper, the truth might be revealed.

However, for this to work, she would need to make sure Lady Beaumont was alone.

Tiptoeing out of the kitchen, Mary listened carefully as she walked down the corridor, hesitating as she heard the loud chime of the grandfather clock in the passage, ringing out the hour of eight p.m.

The parlor door was ajar. She couldn't hear any voices coming from within, but listening carefully, she heard the soft flip and shuffle of cards.

Mary concluded that meant Lady Beaumont was in the parlor alone, and that Maxwell must be out. As was her custom when she dined alone, the lady would now be having an after-dinner drink, and most likely, playing a game of patience at the card table.

That gave Mary the chance she needed. Desperate times called for desperate measures.

Taking a deep breath, with her questions ready in her mind, she tapped on the parlor door and then boldly walked inside.

CHAPTER TWELVE

Lady Beaumont looked up sharply as soon as Mary entered the parlor, and Mary noted the suspicion in her eyes.

"I don't need anything, thank you," she said crisply, dismissing Mary before she'd even reached the dark blue rug. "You may go." She paused. "Why are you even on duty? This is your early day, isn't it?"

She paused, in a meaningful way. Without a doubt, the events of yesterday were on her mind. Now, Mary was curious to know why she hadn't yet mentioned them.

"Yes, my lady, it is my early day," Mary said, but she didn't leave, as Lady Beaumont had hinted for her to do. Instead, she crossed the rest of the way over the carpet and stood politely in front of the red velvet armchair where Lady Beaumont was seated. The lady was wearing her eyeglasses and had a cup of tea in her right hand. Cards were arranged on the table in front of her, together with an empty cognac glass.

"So, why are you here?" The lady took a sharp breath. "Is this about this – this murder? I have been reserving judgment on it, and haven't felt ready to speak to you. But I am extremely disturbed by it. I can see in your eyes that there's something wrong. Have you come to confess? Did you do this out of – out of misguided loyalty?"

"No, my lady," Mary said, her mind racing as she tried to plot out the best way forward through these uncharted waters. Interrogating one's employer? That was definitely not covered in the "How to Succeed as a Housemaid" rulebook. Especially since Lady Beaumont was now in the process of interrogating her.

Mary reminded herself she hadn't always been a housemaid. She'd started her working career in the tough, harsh factory environment, filling in for the men. Although the workplace had been very rough and ready, the girls had always spoken up when they'd felt something was wrong. After all, when working with heavy machinery, not speaking up about a problem might mean getting injured or crushed.

Now, she drew on that outspoken strength of character as she faced down her imperious employer.

"I'd like to make sure about something, if you don't mind, my lady," she said.

"What's that?" Now, Lady Beaumont's voice was tense.

"I couldn't help overhearing people talking earlier today, in the village."

"And what did they say?" The lady put down her cup with a clink into the gold-rimmed china saucer. Hoping for some inspiration, Mary stared around at the walls, before meeting that piercing gaze again.

The walls had paintings of stern-faced men and women, sitting in ornate chairs or else, astride high quality horses. These must be the Beaumonts' actual ancestors, Mary thought. She noticed a resemblance. Knowing that she was being scrutinized by the bygone generations didn't make this any easier.

"People were saying that there was – well, some very bad blood between yourself and the – er – deceased judge, Harold Thompson."

Lady Beaumont's face hardened in a way that told Mary she was ready for battle.

"And you're believing idle village gossip as fact?" she stated incredulously.

"My lady," Mary endeavored to explain, "the police are questioning me about this. Constable Davies is believing outright lies that he's been told about me. I don't know what other rumors are circulating, but I was hoping that you might explain if there was some difficulty between you and Harold Thompson? Was there anything that happened in the past?"

From Lady Beaumont's face, it was clear that she was utterly shocked by Mary's impertinence.

"This is unbelievable," the lady muttered. "You come in here, into my own parlor, and start questioning me as if you were the constable and I was a housemaid suspected of murder! Never have I imagined such a thing could happen!"

"I didn't mean to sound forward or impertinent," Mary said apologetically. "I just wanted to find out the truth."

In the past, she'd thought that Lady Beaumont had been more approachable than the average upper class landowner. But Mary wondered now if that had just been the mantle she'd worn. Now it was stripped away, she saw no willingness to cooperate in her expression at all. Lady Beaumont looked angry and affronted, and she frowned, adjusting her spectacles to glare at Mary more piercingly.

"The truth is that Harold Thompson is an odious man. I know wha he's capable of, but I chose to ignore it. And as for you, I will not have this level of disrespect taking place in my household. You will go Now! And it is not your place to ask any questions of anybody in this house! If I see you are persisting in doing so, then I will personally cal the police, and have you removed!"

Her voice was so sharp, Mary was surprised it hadn't shattered one of the parlor's big bay windows. And the threat was real. There was nothing for it but to retreat, at once.

"I'm sorry if you found my questioning impertinent, my lady," she said quietly. Then she turned and walked out of the room. She hurried all the way to the end of the corridor, and rounded it, before letting ou a deep sigh and leaning against the wall.

Maybe that had been a little forward, but Lady Beaumont's defensiveness seemed to be disproportionate. Why had she become so furious? She'd shared her opinion of Harold, but then, why had she instantly forbidden Mary from talking to anyone?

There were secrets surrounding the conflicted relationship between the Beaumonts and Harold Thompson.

Even if Lady Beaumont had not killed Harold herself, Mary was certain that she held a clue to this mystery. Now, how was she going to find it?

As Mary puzzled over that thought, she heard gravel scrunching from outside the front door.

Hurrying to a window in the corridor, she peered out. Right now the atmosphere in this house felt volatile and she needed to keep track of who was arriving.

To her shock, she saw Constable Davies climbing out of the car The constable's graying hair glimmered in the glow from the outside lantern before he took his helmet off the passenger seat and placed it on his head. He tugged at his jacket, straightening it up before marching to the front door.

Mary's heart went into overdrive.

Her questioning of Lady Beaumont couldn't have happened at a worse time. The constable would find her angry and ready to tell him exactly what Mary had asked her. That could go very badly for her.

She waited, pressed against the wall, listening out nervously, as the butler went to answer the door.

"Good evening." The constable's loud, rasping tones resounded in the evening stillness. "Is Lady Beaumont in? I would like to confirm some facts with her."

Confirm facts? With the lady who was now as mad as a wet hen?

What facts did he want to confirm? That was the question Mary was now asking.

His footsteps tramped down the corridor, and then Mary heard muted voices, and the click of the parlor door closing.

She waited until the butler's footsteps had retreated, and then she tiptoed down the corridor and pressed her ear to the door, hoping that she might pick up on the reason for the constable's visit, and what these facts were.

Maybe he'd also found out about this bad blood. He could be here to question Lady Beaumont as a suspect, and not here about Mary at all.

But to Mary's disappointment, the parlor door was too thick to hear clearly through it, and this conversation was too muted.

Both Constable Davies and Lady Beaumont were both talking in low voices. That was highly unusual, Mary thought. The times that the constable had spoken to her, it had felt like a foghorn was blaring at her. He hadn't lowered his voice in the slightest, and had trumpeted out his suspicions about her guilt, for all to hear.

Maybe it was just another example of double standards of treatment.

For just a moment, she picked up Lady Beaumont's voice, raised in what sounded like a brief flare of emotion. And finally, Mary heard one word clearly.

Maxwell.

After that, the voices died down to the merest mutter.

Maxwell? Had the policeman had come here, late at night, asking about him?

Maybe the feud between the Beaumonts and Harold Thompson had been carried forward by the son. In fact, Maxwell could have done what Lady Beaumont might have hesitated to do.

Knowing this, what should she do next?

She wasn't going to be able to investigate Maxwell alone. It would be too risky. She'd need a lookout and a partner for this dangerous foray into the son's private rooms.

Crossing fingers that Hannah was still awake, Mary tiptoed away from the parlor door, and turned in the direction of her bedroom, her thoughts preoccupied with all the shocking facts she'd learned today.

"Hannah!" Mary whispered her friend's name as she opened the bedroom door, relieved that the bedside lamp was glowing, and that Hannah was not asleep.

In fact, she was sitting up in bed, propped against her pillows, with a tray balanced on her knees.

Hannah was – writing?

"What are you doing?" Mary asked, temporarily distracted from the urgency of her own situation.

"I'm writing a letter," Hannah said, in patient tones that told Mary she was stating the obvious.

The obvious, yes, but not all of it.

"To your mum?" Mary asked. She normally wouldn't have asked. The only reason she was asking was because there had been a strangely secretive note in Hannah's voice.

"No," Hannah said cagily. She glanced up at Mary, who saw to her surprise that Hannah's cheeks were a lot redder than usual.

There were wheels within wheels here. Her mind went back to the moment on that holiday, where she and Gilbert had been standing on the beach, deep in conversation. Mary had heard a familiar laugh coming from behind one of the beach houses. She'd glanced in that direction and had seen Hannah stroll out, chatting in an animated way to a young man.

Mary's impression of him was that he was tall, sturdy, and that he'd been enjoying the conversation as much as Hannah had been. But then, her focus had returned to Gilbert. Every precious moment with him, on the beach, had mattered to her, and she'd put the questions about Hannah out of her mind.

Now, they were flooding back.

"Is that the man you met when we were at the seaside?" she asked, grinning, suddenly feeling as if the day had taken a more cheerful turn.

"It might be, yes," Hannah replied, giving Mary a sidelong glance.

"Well! Hannah, that's – that's wonderful! I only glimpsed you together, but I thought you were really getting along."

"We had a few good conversations," Hannah admitted, her cheeks still pink. "And now, we're continuing them via correspondence."

Mary plonked herself down on the bed next to her friend, so that the springs bounced, causing Hannah to frown at her in mock disapproval

71

as she quickly snatched her pen away from the page. "So. What's his name?"

"His name is Oscar," Hannah said. "Stop bouncing like that! You're going to make my writing squiggly!"

"And? What does he do?"

"He's a hotel manager. He manages a small seaside inn, about a mile away from where we were staying. It's fun but challenging, he says."

"I'm thrilled," Mary said. "I'm so happy for you. Hannah, I hope that you get to see him again."

She shrugged. "I guess it depends. I'm just a maid. I don't know where I'll be working next. So – yes. That's not a given."

The sudden flatness in her voice reminded Mary poignantly of their circumstances. Housemaid work was hard, and long hours, and when it came to pursuing a romance, it was most definitely limiting. A lot of maids ended up having relationships with footmen or stable hands on the same property, purely because those were the only people they got to see regularly.

"But anyway," Hannah said, closing the notebook and pushing her tray away. "Let's not worry about me now. Let's focus on clearing your name, shall we? Did you find anything important out today?"

"It was surprise after surprise," Mary admitted, counting on her fingers. "Samuel Blackthorn had an alibi. Clara, his lover, doesn't have an alibi but the constable has questioned her and I guess, cleared her. I overheard somebody gossiping that there's a big vendetta between the Beaumonts and Harold Thompson, and so I've been focusing again on the competition, and Lady Beaumont's possible need to remove that judge permanently."

"Lady Beaumont?" Hannah sounded aghast.

"I confronted her just now," Mary admitted, as Hannah gasped. "It didn't go well. She was furious. But as I left, Constable Davies arrived. He's in with her now, and I heard them mentioning Maxwell's name."

"Hmmm." Hannah tapped her pen against the tray as she considered all the new information. "Now, that's interesting. Did Maxwell do something to help his mother? Or did he have his own reasons for hating Harold Thompson?"

"I remember Maxwell sneaked out on the night he arrived, and he secretly met somebody at the gate," Mary said. "It looked like a very furtive meeting, and he was angry. I think he's up to something. He has things going on that he doesn't want people knowing about. There are too many secrets, Hannah. Here, in the manor house, and in the village."

Hannah nodded wisely. "If we can find out the secrets, then we might find the killer?"

"That's what I'm thinking," Mary said.

"Well, I was listening out today, and asking a few questions while I worked," Hannah updated her. "I did hear that Maxwell seemed to have been in trouble recently. He was meeting a couple of people in the village, seeming desperate and frantic, but nobody could tell me why. And people were referring to a big fight that Lady Beaumont recently had, although I didn't get the name of the person she fought with. But it does seem that there's a lot more to their situation than we guessed."

"How are we going to find out more?" Mary asked.

She and Hannah stared at each other.

"I thought we were all done with looking in people's rooms." Hannah's voice was thoughtful.

"That was before we found out how many secrets the Beaumonts have," Mary said.

Hannah sighed. "It seems like we're going to be risking jail every time we try to find anything out. Why couldn't this be simpler? But it looks like the only way of learning what Maxwell knows is to have a snoop inside his study."

Mary nodded. "Exactly what I'm thinking." She tried to quell the nerves that were swirling inside her at the thought of another illegitimate search.

"We can say we're cleaning, if anyone walks in," Hannah said.

"Exactly. Cleaning."

"What time does Maxwell usually go down for breakfast?" Hannah glanced at the small clock on the shelf.

"If I remember rightly, he breakfasts quite early, at about eight."

"Then – eight it is. Better get your work done fast tomorrow morning, so we've got some time to go in there and uncover those secrets."

CHAPTER THIRTEEN

The familiar sound of the grandfather clock chiming the hour of eight rang in Mary's ears the next morning as she sneaked along the passage that led to Maxwell's rooms. From the opposite side, she saw Hannah approaching, tiptoeing along, checking behind her every couple of paces.

"He's definitely down at breakfast," she whispered, when she reached Mary. "I saw him going into the dining room about ten minutes ago."

"Right. We need to work quietly, and we need to work fast."

Mary had brought along a feather duster to justify her presence in the study, which was positioned across the corridor from Maxwell's bedroom. Wielding it in a determined way, she opened the door and they stepped inside.

"If we hear him coming back, you leave," she said to Hannah quietly as they entered. "You leave, and I pretend to be dusting. Right?"

"Right," Hannah replied, her voice wobbling.

The study was dark, with the thick, heavy curtains drawn, and the smell of polished wood, with an undertone of paper, filled the air. Mary's heart pounded as she sneaked across the room and drew one of the curtains back, so that a ray of sunlight brightened the room.

Now she could see the enormous mahogany desk, and the comfortable looking leather chair, and the bookshelves that lined the opposite wall.

"The desk first," Mary said. This was all recent. If Maxwell had been interacting with Harold and things had gone bad, she expected that the correspondence would not be filed away in one of the folders she saw, under a pile of novels, on the second shelf of the bookcase.

It would be in one of the wooden trays on the desk itself.

Mary moved quickly to one of the trays. Hannah took the other. And for a moment, the only sound was the rustle of paper as Mary worked feverishly through the documents.

"There are a lot of bank statements here," she whispered. "And to me, they're all showing a positive balance. It seems like Maxwell must be doing well with this trading."

"I'm seeing something different," Hannah whispered back. "In this tray, I'm seeing a lot of deposits. People in the village have been giving him money to invest. That's what this looks like."

"Maybe Harold invested money with him?" Now the cogs were turning in Mary's mind and the situation was starting to make sense. "Maybe Harold wanted his money back, and Maxwell got angry and refused to pay him, and he…"

But at that stage, her musings were interrupted by the sound of approaching footsteps.

Mary's heart jumped into her throat. Maxwell was coming back, far earlier than they'd expected.. And he was walking so fast that they wouldn't have time to get away. She'd thought there would be time and had an escape route in mind. Now, his brisk footsteps were putting a stop to that idea.

Mary had only one thought in her mind, and that was to protect Hannah. Her friend did not deserve to be caught up in this and have her life ruined.

"Under the desk!" she hissed, grabbing Hannah's shoulder and tugging her down. She would be out of sight there – for a few moments, at least. And then, as the door handle rattled, Mary grabbed the duster and leaped to the other side of the room, brandishing it in the direction of the nearby armchair as the door swung open.

"What the hell?" Maxwell's startled shout filled the room. "What on earth are you doing in here?"

"Good – good morning, sir," Mary said politely. "Just dusting."

"Dusting?" Maxwell's voice rose incredulously. "Don't you know this study is out of bounds? It's usually locked! The only reason I didn' lock it is that I went to grab some breakfast! Then I realized I'd left it open and came back upstairs to lock it. And here I find you – inside?"

"I didn't know it was out of bounds, sir. I'm so sorry."

This was looking like far deeper trouble than she'd feared. If Maxwell walked around that desk and found Hannah there, then she could only guess at the explosion that would follow.

But it Maxwell had other ideas. With a face like thunder, he grabbed the two trays of documents off the desk, turned, shoved them into the wooden cupboard on the far wall, and locked it, before yanking out the key.

Then, he marched back to the study door.

"You can stay in here," he declared. "I'm calling my mother. I want her to see that you were in here – and then, I want her to fire you!"

He slammed the door behind him, and once again, Mary heard the metallic click of the key as it turned.

For a few moments, there was only resounding silence as his footsteps retreated.

This had ended up worse than Mary could possibly have feared. Her daring foray into Maxwell's study had given them only an enticing hint of information before the situation had backfired in the worst way possible.

She couldn't save herself now, but she had to save her friend.

Bending down, she met Hannah's anxious gaze from under the desk.

"You have to get out!" Mary hissed.

"Out?" Sounding incredulous, Hannah scrambled up from under the desk. "No, Mary! For a start, there's no way out. And secondly, I can't leave you to take all the trouble. Fair's fair, we have to share. You're already a murder suspect. Let me take the blame for this."

Mary shook her head. She wasn't going to negotiate. Not when her friend's future was at stake.

"Maxwell has no idea you were in here. He never saw you. They suspect me! It's for the better if you get out. At least you won't be under suspicion – or fired, even if I am."

"I don't mind being fired along with you."

"I'm not having that on your record, when you were helping me."

"But Mary, the door is locked!" Hannah waved her arms violently as if to emphasize this non-negotiable point. Mary felt like waving hers right back again. Her friend was wasting time. At any moment, two sets of footsteps might return, and then it would be too late.

"You can't let them see you here!"

"They'll find me if I go back under the desk. Going back under the desk will land me in worse trouble, too!"

She was right. At this pressured time, hiding was not an option. The Beaumonts would undoubtedly walk around the desk. Mary could visualize Lady Beaumont choosing to sit there while she pronounced her housemaid's fate.

"There's always the window," Mary said firmly. "You can escape out of that."

"But we – we're on the second floor!" Hannah said, turning pale.

"There's a big drainpipe running down this side of the house," Mary encouraged her. "I noticed it when sweeping the courtyard. And below the drainpipe is a soft, freshly dug flower bed. It'll be like landing on a feather mattress, and it'll be a million times better than getting into trouble here!"

"I don't like heights," Hannah muttered, as Mary ushered her over to the window, opened the curtain wider, and slid it open. The fresh, warm air billowed in, bringing a hint of lavender and rose with it. Leaning out of the window, Mary took stock of the situation. She didn't want Hannah to have to do anything death-defying in her efforts to get away, but she *did* want her to get away.

The drainpipe ran to the left of the window, and below the window there was an artistically carved stone ridge. That would work well for Hannah to put her feet on, Mary reasoned. It wasn't too far down to the ground. Maybe a three-yard drop? The room below this was a storage room with a low ceiling.

"See?" Mary encouraged her. "It'll be easy. You'll get out of here and Maxwell will never even know you were inside. No matter what trouble I get into, at least you'll be free and clear."

"I want to support you," Hannah jutted her jaw, but with a hand on her friend's shoulder, Mary shook her head.

"Trust me, you don't want the trouble I'm in. Sliding down a drainpipe will be easy by comparison. And then, at least, you'll still be able to work on this case. I might be arrested after this – or fired. I'll need you here to keep on providing insider information." The threats weighed heavy on her shoulders. She did not want Hannah to get caught up in the explosion that would follow.

"Alright," Hannah squared her shoulders. "I'll do it!"

"Quickly!" Mary implored. They were running out of time. She could hear footsteps coming up the stairs. Two sets. Sounding like they were full of intent.

"Go!"

Taking a deep breath, Hannah scrambled out of the window, got her feet on the ledge, and grasped the drainpipe with both her hands.

"Eeek! It's a long way down!" she whispered.

"Pretend – pretend you're a fireman!" Mary encouraged her. "They slide down poles all the time."

"It seems like there might be a need to put out fires soon, in this study," Hannah said darkly.

"That's my worry, not yours," Mary exhorted her.

Finally, Hannah began slowly sliding down the smoothly painted drainpipe.

She had a good grip on the pipe and looked like she was going to make it safely. At least that was one less thing to worry about, Mary thought, tugging the window down and closing the curtain again.

But, as the door unlocked, and she heard Lady Beaumont's irate voice, saying, "What has she done *now*?" Mary knew her worries were about to multiply.

Trouble had her squarely in its cross-hairs.

CHAPTER FOURTEEN

"What is the meaning of this?"

Mary swallowed as Lady Beaumont's irate voice cut the air like a whiplash. The lady was furious. Her shoulders were tense, her nostrils were flaring, and her eyes were narrowed.

"Mother, it's unacceptable!" Standing behind her in the doorway, Maxwell sounded almost as angry as his mother. "She said she was dusting in here! I don't know how she even found that door open. I always keep it locked. I just didn't bother because I was heading down to breakfast."

"What a pity that Constable Davies is not here right now," Lady Beaumont said.

Mary didn't think it was a pity.

It was just about the only thing that had gone right today. If the constable had chosen to visit Lady Beaumont this morning, instead of last night, she was sure that she would be leaving in handcuffs, in the back of his car.

As it was, she stood nervously beside the leather armchair, still clutching her duster, as if it gave her some validation for being here.

"I had no idea the study was out of bounds, my lady," she said calmly. "I mean, Mr. Beaumont has barely been here since I started working and I wasn't told. I was on my way to tidy his room while he was at breakfast, and thought I should quickly pop in here and do some dusting."

That wasn't true, and how she hated having to lie. At least the duster confirmed her rather shaky excuse.

But Maxwell was glowering at her, his expression darkening.

"Mother," he said, "I'm not happy about having this maid working here. I don't trust her!"

"You're right, son," Lady Beaumont said, her mouth tightening again. "I've had issues with this maid before now. She walked into the parlor last night and began asking me the most impertinent questions. I do not trust her any longer, but I am not prepared to go so far as calling her a criminal."

Well, that was a relief. At least Lady Beaumont was being fair-minded, a quality that Mary had noticed in her before.

Although it could be that the reason she knew Mary wasn't a killer was that she knew her son was.

Maxwell's eyes widened.

"Mother, I deal with confidential issues in my work!" he protested. "How can you have somebody working for you that you don't trust? I don't want her looking through my things."

Lady Beaumont hesitated. "You don't think you're being unreasonable? She's only got a few more days left here."

"I don't want her in this house anymore," Maxwell insisted. "In fact, can't you call the police back again? I think that Constable Davies should arrest her immediately!"

Mary fought to remain calm as Maxwell pressured his mother. Panicking now wouldn't help. If she could remain innocent and dignified, then hopefully Lady Beaumont would stick to her guns and not call the police.

"The police are not available this morning," Lady Beaumont said. "I believe the constable is spending this morning investigating a petty theft in a neighboring village," Lady Beaumont said. "That is why he came past last night to confirm some facts. It's a shame to see this surge of crime in what was such a peaceful place, stretching our poor constabulary to their limits."

"A real shame," Maxwell said, staring at Mary with dislike. "Still, when she's locked up, I'm sure the surge in crime will abate."

"It's possible, but we must wait for the law to run its course," Lady Beaumont said, still remaining neutral and not taking her son's side.

Mary took a deep breath, bravely meeting their combined stares. It was time to speak up for herself, difficult as this was going to be.

"I know how this must look to you," she said. "But the truth is, I'm not the killer. I have no idea why Harold Thompson was murdered, but I am starting to think that it's a much more complex situation than I first thought. And the problem is that so many people in this village seem to have secrets."

She started from Lady Beaumont to Maxwell. And to her surprise, she saw Maxwell's cheeks redden deeply. That comment had hit home. Quickly, she continued.

"I'm sorry for having come into your study. I understand if you don't want me to work here anymore. But I'm no killer, and just because

I'm the new person in town doesn't mean I am willing to be accused of a crime I didn't commit."

"You have no right to go prying into anybody's secrets," Maxwell said, completely ignoring most of Mary's heartfelt words. "Mother, fire her!"

Lady Beaumont sighed, squaring her shoulders, and Mary knew that the words she'd dreaded were coming.

"I am sorry to have to do this, Mary Adams," she announced "However, circumstances give me no other option. Kindly leave these premises immediately, and I forbid you to return! I believe the police need you to stay in the village, so I suggest you find alternative lodgings at the local inn, until they have finished the investigation."

While Maxwell nodded supportively, Mary did the only thing she could. With her head lowered, she walked out of the room, feeling the waves of resentment from Maxwell Beaumont lashing her as she passed.

What a debacle! Now she'd been thrown out of the manor house and Maxwell would be keeping his study firmly locked and his secrets hidden away. Whatever was in those trays, Hannah wouldn't get a second look at it.

Yet again, she'd been so close to finding out something important she was convinced of it.

Dispiritedly, she headed to her room, leaving a note for Hannah.

"I've been fired. I'm going to get a room in the village inn for now Please come and find me when you can."

Then she packed up her belongings into her heavy bag and shunted it downstairs.

It was a long, arduous walk from the front door, where the butler stared at her disapprovingly, to the main gate. Her bag was heavy, and it wasn't easy to carry. But she'd have to press on because it was another mile to the inn.

Step by step, with her back and arms starting to ache, Mary inched her way down the narrow road. The shame of being fired was still burning inside her, and unfortunately, there was no denying that she had been looking where she shouldn't.

But what had Maxwell been hiding? The transactions that Hannah had seen had sounded very strange. Was there a connection with Harold Thompson, and if so what was it?

Did his mother know about it?

As she tried to replay that pressured search in her mind, Mary became aware of a sound behind her.

It was the roar of a car's engine, approaching fast.

Very fast. For a moment, she'd wondered if she could flag this car down and get a ride to the inn – after all, the road went directly to the village. She quickly realized the car was coming too fast for that, and in fact, it was speeding up.

A little voice inside Mary's head told her, "Trouble's coming!"

She swung around to take a look at the car and saw, to her astonishment, that it was veering directly toward her.

No time to see who was behind the wheel. All she could tell, in her state of panic, was that the car was big, intimidating, and dark-colored.

Someone was trying to run her down! And in another heartbeat, that car would crash straight into her.

CHAPTER FIFTEEN

With only a moment to spare, Mary dived into the hedge, branches scratching and scouring her face and arms. She heard the scream of tires as the car sped past, the crackle of branches as it sideswiped the hedge, and a rush of air as it passed, missing her by inches. And then finally, there was a thud and a squish as it ran over her bag.

Then, with a belch of exhaust fumes, it was gone.

Feeling utterly shaken, with scratches on her arms and face and leaves entangled in her hair, Mary extricated herself from the hedge. She was shaking with reaction. That had been a close call. The driver had intended to get her. He, or she, had been aiming for her.

And he, or she, had run over her bag!

There was now a big tire imprint, a squashed section, and a rip in the canvas. Some of her clothes were spilling out, and one of her books looked to have been totally mangled.

The car had disappeared, veering around a bend in the road, before she'd had a chance to properly look at it, never mind see the driver.

The driver had intended to hit her. She was sure of it. That driver had recognized her. This had been deliberate and opportunistic, and she felt as if there was a target painted on her back now.

Hearing another engine from behind her, Mary flinched nervously, ready for another headlong dive into the hedge. But the rattling jalopy that came into view was a farm vehicle, traveling at a quarter of the speed. And in response to her frantic waving, it stopped.

"Need a ride to town?" the driver asked, leaning over and opening the door as he adjusted his tweed cap.

"Yes, please," she said. Just as well he'd offered, because her bag was about to break apart. Her trusty canvas holdall, which she'd resented many a time for its size and weight, was now half-obliterated.

If she was going to move on anywhere else, she'd need to buy a new one.

Somehow, she managed to cram the bag in front of the seat, bending down to pick up a pair of socks that had dropped out through the gash.

The farm worker didn't comment, just whistled gently through his teeth. And, as she sat gingerly on the seat, which contained a very dirty headcollar and lead rope, a saddle cloth that had seen better days, and a leaky tube of horse liniment, Mary realized that he wasn't even noticing her broken bag.

As soon as she'd slammed the door, he got going again, and they chugged at a slow and deliberate pace into town.

He pulled up outside the inn, and Mary thanked him profusely as she lifted her battered bag out, strewing socks on the sidewalk once more.

"No problem at all, young miss. Glad to help," he said, before driving away.

Mary shunted her bag inside, and delved into one of the side pockets to remove her meager savings as she headed for the reception desk and asked if they had a single room.

"We do, on the third floor," the well-groomed receptionist said, looking dubiously at Mary's bag.

The room was surprisingly expensive. She couldn't stay here more than one night without seriously depleting the nest egg she'd worked so hard to build.

That meant she had a lot to do today.

The room might be expensive, but after she'd dragged her bag up the stairs, Mary found it was spacious and clean, cool and airy, and the bed was comfortable. Also, the window overlooked the street, and staring down, Mary took in the view of the village. Someone in this peaceful, idyllic place had just tried to kill her. If she hadn't dived out of the way, she would be flattened on the road.

Now that she was in a quiet space where she could think, Mary tried her best to replay the incident.

The biggest and most pressing question was: had this killer been either of the Beaumonts?

She didn't think so. The reason was that the driveway had been visible from the road, and she hadn't heard or seen a car coming down it. She didn't think that car had been Maxwell's. He drove a sporty, white model, and this one had definitely been bigger and dark in color.

Could it have been Clara?

Mary wasn't ruling that out. It might have been. But whoever the driver had been, she was sure they had seen and recognized her.

If they had tried to run her down, that meant they had been keeping track of what she was doing, and they knew she was asking questions.

"You need to think of it as being a positive," she told herself. "If you're close to finding the killer, and they're threatened by what you've been doing, that's a good thing, right?"

The problem was that she still had no idea who the killer was!

They might think she knew, but she didn't.

Mary stood up, feeling suddenly restless, and paced the room. This was the most frustrating situation. None of the villagers were willing to talk, and every time she thought she'd opened a door, it was slammed in her face before she got a proper look inside.

How could she make progress before Constable Davies came around to the inn and took her away?

Thinking furiously, Mary paced again. There had to be a way of finding out these secrets and learning how they were all linked. She was sure they were linked, and that what she'd done so far had given her a peek into them.

With dead ends trapping her in every direction, Mary couldn't shake off a feeling of nervous doom. It was clear that there had to have been a killer. That champagne bottle had not dropped on Harold Thompson's head accidentally. But what if this was one of those crimes that could never be solved?

Cold cases, that was what they were called. She knew that from the reading she'd done, although in her detective books, cases never went cold. The sleuth, or the policeman, always solved them in a flash of brilliance.

But this was real life, and to avoid this case going cold, there was only one obvious suspect at the present time. Herself. It was no wonder that Constable Davies was targeting her with such inexorable intent.

What hadn't she done? What could she do to find out more?

As she fretted, staring out of the inn's window at the summery sky which was looking far too cheerful and bright for such a serious time, Mary had an idea.

"Wait a minute!" she said aloud, thinking back to the fateful afternoon of that judging. At the time she needed it most, she realized who might have the answers. "I know who I must question next – and he must know something, even if he doesn't realize it!"

CHAPTER SIXTEEN

A snippet of speech was coming back to Mary, a conversation she'd overheard at the start of the judging. The competition organizer had welcomed the obnoxious judge, and Harold Thompson rudely said that although he'd judged at many other events, this was the first time his local village had appointed him.

Now that Mary was replaying that conversation in her mind, she thought it was significant.

Why would the judge have been appointed this time? Had someone wanted him there, despite his rudeness and his reluctance to give out any prizes at all?

In her mind, the puzzle pieces were now starting to fit together.

Perhaps the killer had planned for him to be invited to the gathering, knowing that he'd be alone in the judges' tent after the last event of the day. And if so, the competition organizer. He would hold the key to this.

Perhaps, as the organizer, he was the one who had invited Harold Thompson deliberately, and if so, when she got face to face with him, she'd be staring the killer in the eye.

Or else, he might have been asked to do so by somebody influential in the village. If Mary could dig deep enough to find that out, then she'd uncover the killer's name.

There wasn't a moment to lose. She now needed to work out who this organizer was and where he lived.

Had his name been mentioned? Mary thought it had. She had seen his name tag. What had it said? Thinking hard, she tried to remember.

Mr. Smythe. Patrick Smythe. That was his name. He'd been a sturdy man, of below average height and above average width. He'd had a good natured face, but with a nervous expression which now made sense. He'd also been perspiring a lot. Yes, the day had been hot, and his dark suit must have been overly warm, but sweating was also a sign of nervousness and unease. Maybe he'd guessed what trouble would explode when this unpopular judge announced his results.

Now that she'd remembered Patrick Smythe's name, the question was where to find him.

Hopefully, seeing the gathering weekend was now over, he'd be relaxing at home. All she needed to do was find out his address, and for that, she decided this time she would see if she got any luck from the local telephone directory.

If she could sneak unobtrusively past the post office, there was a telephone kiosk next door to it, and there would be a directory inside it.

The first step was to change her clothes. Mary decided that an inconspicuous outfit was the order of the day. It might not stop this killer from recognizing her, but hopefully it would slow him down if he, or she, met her on the road.

She decided on the trousers she'd worn yesterday, paired with a gray top and a small but chic sun hat in cream.

With a new outfit, and her hair tied into a tight ponytail so it wouldn't attract the killer's eye, she headed downstairs, and walked down the main road until she reached the post office. It was now lunchtime, and the village was quiet and sleepy. There were only a couple of cars on the road, and none of the drivers gave her as much as a glance.

Walking into the telephone kiosk, Mary saw it had what she needed – the rather slim directory which contained information for the three local villages, as well as the bigger town that was their central point.

She paged through, guessing that even in a smaller village, there might be more than one Smythe. Sure enough, when she reached the S section, she saw there were several.

She ran her finger down the list, hoping she could identify the right one, when a tapping from behind her nearly made her heart jump right out of her throat.

Whirling around, losing her place in the directory as it fell shut, she found herself confronted by an irate looking elderly lady, of about seventy-five years old, with a cloud of gray hair and a stern expression.

"Young lady," she said, "what are you doing in there? Are you simply wasting time? I have to telephone my daughter on the hour! She is expecting me to call at lunchtime."

"Er – I'm terribly sorry."

No point at all in trying to argue with this elderly grand dame that it was a public telephone. In this small village, the grand dame clearly believed that it was *her* telephone, when the hour struck at least.

"I'll be one minute." With a stressed smile, Mary flipped the pages back again, finding the place she'd lost.

There it was! Smythe, P. He lived at number 3 Begonia Avenue, which was just down the road. Not that this was surprising, because in this village, everything was down the road.

"Thank you," Mary said, stepping out of the kiosk and getting a stern nod from the elderly lady.

"Don't do it again!" she warned Mary as she stepped inside.

Shaking her head ruefully at the entitlement of the village elders, Mary hurried in the direction of Begonia Avenue, and headed down it, seeing that number three was toward the end of the road, and close to the village pub.

The houses on this road had bigger gardens than the average, and they were beautifully cared for, with well-tended beds, colorful flowers, and mowed grass. She passed one house that featured a scenic swing under a spreading oak tree, another with a bed of chrysanthemums that were blazing with red, pink and white colors, and another where the owner had created an ornamental fishpond, with a stone bench placed beside it. He was sitting on the bench, in the shade of a tree, reading a book.

When she was still two houses away, Mary saw the door of number three swing open.

She sped up, worrying that she was too late, and that the organizer was going to climb into the shiny Range Rover parked outside the gate, and be gone.

At least she could see this was the organizer. Even looking at his back view, she recognized that sturdy build, those broad shoulders, the way he had of walking which was slightly labored, as if the air was thicker for him than it was for a normal person, and he had to push his way through it.

He trod down the path, and just as she was about to call out to him, hoping to attract his attention before he climbed into his car, she saw that he wasn't heading for his car at all.

With his heavy-footed walk, he was making his way toward the local pub.

It would have been easier to speak to him in the privacy of his home than in a more public setting, where he might have friends around him. One on one was always better in these situations, she knew from experience.

But if he was the killer, then a public place would be safer. There was always that to think about, Mary told herself, looking for the bright side.

Determinedly, she sped up, arriving at the pub just a minute after him. She waited at the door, watching as he took the large, golden glass of beer which the barmaid had already poured for him. Carrying it carefully, he went to sit at a corner table below a gold-framed print of racehorses sprinting for the finish line.

The pub was quiet and the lunch time rush had not yet descended. Perhaps it didn't descend at all on a Monday, and people went there for an early dinner instead. The atmosphere inside was peaceful, smelling of smoke and stale beer, with a faint tinge of fried fish and chips. Apart from the barmaid, who looked at her inquiringly, the only other customers were two middle aged men who were deep in conversation over beers that were already three quarters empty.

Mary headed to the counter and ordered herself a sparkling lemonade.

"Here you go," the barmaid said, pouring it for her and adding a straw and a slice of lemon.

Taking the drink, Mary carried it to the corner table, where Patrick Smythe was sipping his beer thoughtfully, staring across the bar with a serious expression on his heavy-jowled face.

"Good afternoon, Mr. Smythe," she said politely.

He looked up, startled, slopping some of his beer onto the table. Quickly, he put the glass down.

"Good afternoon – er." He had no idea of her name, but he recognized her face and she saw his gaze sharpen.

"I'm Mary Adams," she admitted. "I was at the festival yesterday when the – the murder took place."

"Wait a minute." Now, he was putting two and two together. "You were that woman! The one who spoke on stage, and then later on, you asked me where the judge was! You went looking for him just before the – the incident. And then, you rushed in and called me."

"That's correct," Mary admitted. "I found him dead."

"You did? I'm wondering about that now." He stared at her with a cynical expression.

"It was so disturbing to me that I'm trying to make sense of it by asking questions, and finding out where everyone else was," Mary explained. "Since you knew where Harold Thompson was, I'm wondering if you might have popped out earlier to see him? Maybe to check he had everything he needed after the judging?"

His eyes widened at this accusation, and he was quick to speak in his own defense.

"I was very busy at the time," he said hastily. "I'd just finished a long meeting with my secretary. We were checking all the results, and then allocating the produce, the jams and the cakes to be sent to various good causes. I didn't seen Harold myself after the competition ended."

Just like that, he'd been kind enough to supply her with an alibi. So she knew he wasn't the killer. Not if he'd been wrapping things up in the pavilion along with his secretary.

"I was wondering something." She leaned closer. Having blurted out his alibi, the competition organizer looked to her as if he'd had his say. He was frowning at her in an irritable way, as if wishing that she would go away and leave him in peace.

"Look," he said, "I'm a busy man. Can this not wait? After the – the extreme stress of the weekend, I am having some quiet time for a few minutes, before a close friend arrives."

"I understand, and I'm sorry," Mary said. "I'm also stressed. It's very stressful to be wrongfully accused of murder, and I want to find the perpetrator. Otherwise, everyone's in danger, aren't they?"

Trying to strike a balance between a polite yet firm approach, Mary tried her best to reason with the competition organizer, in a way that would convince him that his own interests might be at risk if the killer wasn't found.

"What will happen next year if there's an unsolved murder hanging over the festival? It will be very hard to find somebody to judge your competition, if the last judge was killed, and the killer was never found?"

"Well," Smythe said grumpily, "it'll be hard finding *anyone* to enter the competition next year, after the debacle with the judging yesterday. I've already had about ten telephone calls, and two letters of complaint."

Mary had to admit he had a point there. What jam maker would want to be publicly humiliated in that way again? Luckily, this faultlessly logical comment had led her round to where she wanted to go, and that was to ask him why he'd picked Harold in the first place.

"At least Harold Thompson can't judge the competition again," she reassured him.

He gave a grim nod. "At least he can't," he agreed.

"Is it difficult to find people to do the judging?"

He frowned. "Well, it can be a challenge, you know. People don't like the same judge every time, so we've alternated a couple of judges in the past. Competitors do like somebody who's an expert in the field and whose opinion will carry weight."

"And why did you pick Harold?"

That was the key question. Mary was very interested in the answer, especially since Smythe was now fidgeting uncomfortably.

"Well, you know, I was wondering if it might have been an oversight not using him, since he's a pillar of the local community, and all…"

"How long has the festival been running?" Mary asked.

Pride filtered back into his expression now. "This is its fifteenth year in the current format," he said. "It ran before then, but in a much smaller way and without the jam and cake competitions."

"And is this the very first year you've used Harold?"

"It is," Smythe confirmed again.

"Why did you decide to use him?"

But for some strange reason, this question proved to be a stumbling block.

"I – er, well, you know, we can't ignore our local experts forever, ha ha," he said, with a weak attempt at a laugh.

"Did anyone in particular suggest him?"

"No. No. He contacted me, and – er – well, made it clear that he'd like to judge."

Smythe was now turning pink. He took refuge in his beer, draining it deeply. Mary stared at him, feeling perplexed. There were wheels within wheels here, and she was sure that Smythe wasn't telling her everything. There was something strange going on. Why was he looking so uneasy? Why had he now drunk half of a large glass of beer in one gulp?

It seemed that nobody except Harold himself had pressured the organizer into using him, but it definitely seemed that pressure had been exerted.

Knowing that she didn't understand the complexities, but not sure what to ask next, Mary was considering her options when Smythe made it clear that her time was up.

"Young lady," he said, "I find your questions to be distracting, and as I said, I am taking a day off after my hard work this weekend. If you wish to meet with me, kindly contact me during office hours, and we can set up a meeting – the rest of this week is very full, as is next week, but perhaps we can find a date that will work in July. For now, though, I must ask you to leave. I am expecting company any minute."

His voice was firm. And Mary didn't want to cause a scene.

"Thank you," she said politely, before turning and leaving.

Walking out of the bar, into the sunlight that seemed very bright after its dimly lit interior, she puzzled over Patrick Smythe's strange reaction.

It was almost as if he'd been coerced into using Harold. Harold had put pressure on him and demanded to be the judge. Had that just been because he knew the organizers had been avoiding him because he was so unpleasant, and he'd found a way to force Smythe?

Mary didn't know. But what she did know was that Harold had definitely had some kind of strong influence over Patrick Smythe. Strong enough to compel Patrick to let him judge, even though Patrick had probably known it was going to end badly. Had Harold threatened him with some adverse consequences if he didn't let him judge?

What could those consequences be?

But maybe an even better question, Mary reasoned, was whether Harold had held the same sway over anybody else.

Maybe Patrick Smythe wasn't the only one he'd threatened.

And perhaps somebody else had decided to silence those threats, forever.

Thinking of that, Mary realized that it was time to search somebody's home again.

She'd gotten into trouble at every place she'd been to so far.

But there was one place she hadn't been, one site where all the secrets would surely be hidden. And that was in the home of the victim – Harold Thompson himself.

Heading for the main road, with resolve surging inside her, Mary thought that at least, this time, she wouldn't get into trouble from the homeowner. She couldn't, because he was dead.

However, she would need to be very careful and keep all her wits about her as she embarked on this risky activity.

The killer was tracking her – and he, or she, might be watching.

CHAPTER SEVENTEEN

Mary had no idea where Harold Thompson lived, although she knew it was somewhere in the village. Glancing at the phone booth a she passed, she saw it was still occupied by the elderly lady, who wa engrossed in her conversation.

Interrupting her would not go down well. Mary wasn't going to d it and needed to think of another way to find Harold's address. I anybody would know, she decided, it would be the local inn. Since she was currently a customer there, that might be helpful. Hopefully, they' be willing to tell her.

"I wonder if you could help me," she asked the receptionist at the counter, in polite tones. The receptionist was looking tired, as if thi warm afternoon was making her drowsy. She stifled a yawn as she stared out over the lobby, which contained a few chairs, upholstered i deep red leather, and a couple of countryside watercolors on the wall.

Getting closer, Mary saw she'd interrupted her in eating a packet o potato crisps under the desk. The crinkling sound of the wrapper, an the smell of vinegar, was a giveaway.

"What do you want, ma'am?" she asked, trying to summon up polite smile.

"I would like to know where Harold Thompson's house is," Mary said. She decided not to give a reason. It didn't look as if thi receptionist much cared about the reason, although her eyes did wide at the name.

"You know he's…"

"Yes, I know. I just want to know where his house is, that's all."

"It's one of them in Finch Lane," the receptionist said. "But I don' know which one. He never used to come here. Never liked our in much."

It sounded as if Harold didn't like anything much. Thanking her Mary set out in the direction that the receptionist had indicated, keepin, her eyes peeled for approaching cars – and for Finch Lane.

Finch Lane proved to be a most scenic, narrow lane leading off th main road and up a hill to a beautiful forested hilltop.

The trees lining the road were abuzz with birdsong and, Mary thought, the road was well named.

Now to see if she could find out which house was Harold Thompson's. Since there were only a few in the road, all similar charming cottages, she guessed it might require a process of elimination.

There was a car parked outside the first one, and she could see people moving behind the window. That wasn't the place she wanted. She guessed that with the death so recent, his house would be standing empty. After all, his closest relative in the village was his estranged daughter, and she clearly hadn't been in any rush to head to her father's home and pack up his belongings.

Moving on to the second and the third, Mary assessed these charming cottages. One was empty, but it had a note on the door, "Back soon, Terry." The other must have somebody in the back garden, watering the grass. She could see the spray cascading over the colorful flower beds.

There were only two houses left in the row. Would it be this one, up ahead?

Immediately, alarm bells started ringing. For a start, the postbox outside the house – white painted, with a red roof – had a few letters jutting out of it. The door looked firmly locked, but the curtains were not closed.

When Harold had headed out to do his judging, he'd had no idea he wouldn't be returning. Of course, he wouldn't have drawn the curtains when he had believed he'd be back later in the afternoon.

She pulled a letter from the mailbox to make sure, nodding in satisfaction as she saw it was addressed to Mr. H. Thompson.

This was his house. Now to see if she could get inside.

"I'd really rather not break and enter again. Why am I being forced into doing this?" Mary muttered to herself as she sidled up the garden path. If only there was another way to clear her name, but the problem was she couldn't think of one.

Creeping around the house, she tried to dispel the uneasy feeling that she was being watched. Although it was good to be alert, it wouldn't help her to be paranoid. She tried to tell herself nobody was watching and that it was just that after a few bad experiences, she was more nervous than she had been at the start.

Nobody in the countryside locked their kitchen doors when they went out for the day – did they? Hoping that she'd be able to access the house, Mary cautiously tried the kitchen door. Her eyes widened as she realized it was locked.

This was not typical. Harold had something to hide – she was sure of it. Now, would she be able to find another way in?

She inched her way around the house, looking over her shoulder every couple of seconds and making sure to move as quietly as she could.

Here was a small, cozy looking living room, currently bathed in the late morning sun. One of the windows was ajar. Could she pull it wider?

Trying the window, Mary discovered the answer to that was yes. Now to climb inside.

Placing her hands on the sill, she pushed upward and swung her leg over, pleased by how easy it was in the trousers. These were definitely an advantage when it came to illicit breaking and entering.

She landed softly on the carpet, and pushed the window closed again, taking a deep breath as she stared around.

The air in the small living room smelled slightly stale. It had been closed for two full days, and she guessed it didn't take long for that stale smell to start creeping in. But what this told her was that nobody else had been in here, letting fresh air inside the house. Nobody had thought to come here yet, even the police.

Perhaps Constable Davies thought there was nothing to be found in here, but Mary was certain there would be.

From the living room, she headed into a small bedroom. There was a large bed, neatly made, and a nightstand with a couple of papers on it. When she took a closer look, they proved to be old shopping lists. Nothing incriminating or suspicious. Leaving the bedroom, she headed along the passage. There was a kitchen ahead, bright and welcoming, with yellow curtains, but along the way, she passed another closed door.

Opening it, she saw it was a tiny study. There was room only for a desk and chair. The desk was very neat, with nothing except a calendar and an empty jam jar on the top. But how about the drawers?

Mary tried the three desk drawers, frowning in puzzlement as she realized they were locked.

Whatever Harold's secrets were, she was now suspecting they were hidden in here. Who locked their desk drawers, as well as their house? There were too many layers of security here for what she'd expect in a simple countryside cottage.

How to open the drawer?

She wiggled it, but it was firmly locked. The lock did not feel flimsy. It wasn't the kind of drawer that you could pull, thinking it would break. No, this lock was solid and well made.

A nasty thought was occurring to Mary as she straightened up, sighing in annoyance, folding her arms as she turned to look around the room.

What if Harold had kept his desk key with his house key? If he had done that, then the desk key would most likely have been in his pocket or his briefcase, and that meant it would now be in the possession of the police, taken in along with his body.

But Harold seemed like a methodical man, Mary reasoned, trying to find her way past this obstacle that maybe wasn't as immovable as it seemed. He would surely have kept a spare key? He seemed like the kind of well organized man who would have a backup plan in case he mislaid his keys.

If he kept a spare, where would he hide it?

Getting inside the mind of a victim had never been more of an imperative. Mary knew the challenge was on. Could she think like Harold Thompson himself, and could she find the spare key, assuming it existed?

If she'd been Harold, she would have wanted that key within easy reach. He'd seemed like a man who hadn't wanted to waste any time. At any rate, he'd impatiently gotten to the gist of insulting all the jam makers. He hadn't delayed in his attack.

So, that meant he'd be sitting at his desk – maybe she should sit there too?

Taking a deep breath, she pulled out the leather chair and perched on its edge, looking over the expanse of desk, and trying to think uncharitable thoughts about the jam makers and the villagers, just the way Harold might have done.

Had he been left or right handed? Now that she thought back, she realized that he'd been left handed. He'd held the loudspeaker with his left hand, he'd reached out for the teaspoon with his left hand. That was unusual, and it gave her a clue.

It meant that if he'd hidden a key within easy reach, it would have been somewhere he could get to with his left hand, because that would have been more convenient for him.

Pleased with her logic, even though she didn't know if it would produce any results, Mary reached out her left hand and began searching in all the places that a key could easily be hidden.

How about under the rim of the desk? Perhaps that was a bit too easy. She felt there anyway, making a face as she came across a piece of used chewing gum, barely sticky any more, but still unpleasant for fingers to find.

Harold hadn't seemed like a person who'd chew gum and then leave it plastered on the rim of his desk.

Unless – her heart sped up. Unless the gum had been used for the purpose of sticking a key in place. Maybe this was an older hiding place and he'd now found a new one. If that was the case, then all she needed to do was to look for more gum.

She felt around the side of the desk, brushing her fingers over the polished wood. No gum. No key. How about at the bottom? Leaning down as far as she could, she felt along the lower edge of the desk. Nothing there either.

How about the chair? That would be the quickest and easiest of all, surely?

Mary turned her hand the other way, and sent up a little prayer, just in case anyone was listening. Then, she ran her fingers along the underside of the chair's seat.

Nothing – nothing – and then something.

Her index finger touched a large, sticky piece of chewing gum. There was a metal object attached to it. She tugged at it and it came free, and she let out a huge breath of relief.

Finally, she had what she needed. It felt as if, at last, those secrets were within her reach.

Mary slotted the key into the lock and turned it. It unlocked smoothly. Grasping the top drawer, she pulled it open, impatience now surging inside her.

This drawer contained only stationery – some pens, pencils, sharpeners, elastic bands, a handful of coins, and some pound notes in various denominations. Closing the drawer, she went on to the next one.

Here, she found what she needed. She knew it immediately. It was a hardcover, black folder, and on it was a white label. On the label, in jagged capital letters, was printed, PRIVATE.

Private, but not for long, Mary thought, removing the folder, which felt thick and bulky. Just in case, she checked the bottom drawer, but he only thing in there was a clipboard – empty, and a notebook with several blank pages remaining.

The folder was the reason that the drawers had been locked, and now she had it.

With a sigh of relief, she closed the drawer and headed out of the study, shutting the door behind her. At last, she would be able to unlock the unlikeable victim's secrets.

But even as she thought that, Mary heard a sound that made her blood turn to ice.

There were footsteps, scrunching over the gravel path, heading directly for the house. Somebody else was here.

Was it the police? Her heart thudded in her chest as she froze in place. The next moment, a grinding, shearing sound told her otherwise.

Someone was breaking in – forcing the kitchen door. Not the police. They would have keys. There was surely only one person who would need to do this.

She was trapped in the house with the killer.

CHAPTER EIGHTEEN

Rushing down the passageway, clutching the folder to her chest, Mary felt adrenaline pulsing inside her. From behind her, the creak of hinges told her that the kitchen door was opening. The killer was inside. But he'd already tried to kill her once, and if he – or she – found her in here, then the odds were stacked against her survival. She needed to get away.

"Get out, escape, get out." The panicked voice repeated over and over in her mind as she veered into the living room. There was the window. All she had to do was jump through it.

But there wasn't time. The footsteps were coming directly down the corridor. Whoever it was, they were heading straight to the living room themselves.

Had they seen or heard her?

Mary dived behind the couch and pressed herself up against it, trying not to breathe at all as the footsteps neared.

It was ironic, her frightened brain emphasized, that if she were to peek out now, she'd see the killer. But it would be the last thing she saw. No way could she risk moving a muscle. She had to become one with the couch and try not to breathe.

Don't beat so fast, Mary told her heart, but it pounded away in panic, refusing to listen. She held her breath, the blood rushing in her ears.

She could hear him breathing as he looked around the living room just as she had done.

He was looking for the same thing she was. Now, Mary felt certain of it. He'd seen that she was investigating, and he'd decided to break into Harold's house and pre-emptively remove it before she found it!

Only he'd been a minute too late.

The footsteps turned away and headed back down the corridor, and this time, she heard the sound of the study door opening. Just as she'd done, he was now taking a look inside this inconspicuous room.

He wouldn't have the challenge of finding the key, because she'd left it in the desk. He would be able to open the drawers straight away.

and that meant in another few moments, he would see that the folder was not in the only place it could be.

Now, she needed to move fast.

Mary burst from behind the couch and made a rush for the window, trying to keep as quiet as she could, but also trying to move as fast as she was able to. Every moment's delay now made it more likely he'd find her. Already, she could hear the furious slamming of the drawers.

She slung her foot over the sill and leaped out. With the folder firmly in her grasp, clutching it as tightly as she could, she raced around the cottage, heading for the road.

But behind her, there were footsteps, and a wordless, angry cry.

Risking a glance behind her, Mary caught her breath. The killer was wearing a mask! A dark mask, with eyeholes cut in it, obscured his features, and all she could see now was that he was pursuing her with intent.

He wanted to get the folder she had. It contained his secrets. And from the speed at which he was running, Mary knew he also wanted to get *her*.

Could she outrun a long-legged criminal who had everything to lose?

Well, she was going to find out. There was no choice.

As Mary raced down the road, her breath coming fast, she knew she needed to think even faster than she was running. She couldn't keep this pace up. The trousers she'd decided to wear were her saving grace. If it wasn't for them, he'd already have caught up with her. At least they'd allowed her to leap out of the cottage and accelerate up the road.

Her instinct was to flee to the woods and hide, but Mary knew that instinct was badly wrong. It would mean she was alone in a deserted place, and it would be easy for him to find her. She couldn't hide forever in a stretch of woods that he might know well, and she didn't know at all.

No, there was only one way for her to save herself. And that hope rested in the village itself.

The masked man was part of this community, even though she didn't know which part.

But he'd want to keep his motives hidden. Therefore, it was the community that could save her.

So, Mary veered away at the last minute, changing direction. Instead of fleeing uphill, to the perceived safety of the woods, she charged downhill, heading to the next door cottage. She'd spied that glint of water coming from the back garden. There must be a villager there, peacefully watering his lawn, and if she could get to him, then the masked man couldn't follow.

Mary vaulted over the waist-high fence and sprinted into the back garden. She was giving this all she had, and the speed of her running was causing the pages in the folder to slip. Grasping at them, she couldn't prevent a chunk of pages from the back of the folder from slipping to the ground. She gave an anguished grasp, grabbing for them, managing to get all except one, which the breeze tugged away and sent fluttering into the hedge.

No time to get it back, not if she wanted to save herself.

Holding the folder in a renewed, steely grip, Mary ran around the corner of the house, knowing that help would be just a few steps away.

There, she stopped dead, letting out a dismayed cry.

The sprinkler was attached to a hosepipe, which was automatically doing the work, thanks to an ingenious device with small holes drilled in it. Having attached this, the villager was using it to water his lawn, while he went for a walk, or had a nap.

At any rate, he was not in his back garden, and there was no time to summon him from a nap. With a squeak of terror, hearing footsteps thudding behind her, Mary completed a full circle of the lawn. The sprinkler showered over her as she fled past it in a cooling rain. She erupted from the other side of the house, vaulted the fence once more, and carried on along the road. Now, there was no time to waste, because he was closing in. She wouldn't have a chance unless anyone was alert and ready.

How long did it take to kill someone? Only a couple of moments. He might have a weapon with him, an iron bar or a piece of wood. With his mask in place, he could kill her and run away before anyone realized what was happening.

The first house! That was her best hope.

Mary rushed through the open garden gate and down the path. There wasn't even time to knock. She was going to have to hope that the villagers did what she'd assumed everyone living an innocent life in a peaceful place did – and that was to leave their front door open.

Without so much as a knock, Mary flung herself against the front door, wrenching at the handle with her free hand, the one that wasn't still tightly gripping the folder.

It burst open, and Mary tumbled into the entrance hall, tripping over the rug and sprawling headlong.

Astonished cries came from beyond the archway to her right. She heard the smash of a teacup and the tingling sound that indicated a shocked guest had dropped a cake fork.

But she didn't hear the footsteps, following her in. They were retreating fast now, heading back down the road as the masked man rushed for cover, and anonymity.

Mary raised her head.

Four gray haired ladies were looking at her, from around a bridge table, their expressions varying from curiosity, to fear, to shock.

"Goodness me, my dear!" The closest lady clambered to her feet. "What is happening? Are you being chased?"

"That dog on the main road is a biter," the lady opposite her declared, in disapproving tones.

Mary decided, for now, it would be better to underplay this incident. Saying that she was chased by a masked man would undoubtedly result in police being called.

"The dog was very scary," she said. "I thought it safer to run."

"Very wise," one of the other ladies said. "Even though, in those newfangled trousers, I'm sure you'd have been able to get away."

Her voice carried a distinct note of disapproval, in regards to trousers in general, and newfangled ones in particular.

"Don't criticize the young lady," her partner admonished her. "Nowadays, it's all about being equal to the men, isn't it? And if that means she wears the trousers, then good for her."

The gray haired lady was extending a hand, but she was so small and slight that Mary had to get to her feet carefully, to avoid upsetting her balance.

"Can I offer you a cup of tea?" the lady asked.

"No, no thank you. That's very kind. I'll just – just check if that dog's still there."

Returning to the front door, Mary peered out.

There was no sign of the masked man. She didn't know if he had decided to leave the area, or if he was lurking and watching from the cover of the trees. He could try again. This was scary!

Think logically, she told herself.

Since she'd burst into a house containing four curious elderly ladies, she didn't think he would wait around. The wisest course of action would be to leave. It would take him some time to regroup, and that was now the time she had.

"Enjoy your game, and thank you so much for your help," she said breathlessly, to the kindly ladies.

They all nodded proudly, as if her blundering into the house had added an element of excitement to a routine game.

"You take care, my dear," the lady who'd helped her up said.

Mary left, closing the door behind her. Gathering all her courage, she headed down the hill at a speedy walk. The inn was in sight, just a couple of hundred yards away. She could get there without him seeing her. She knew she could.

Even so, it felt like the scariest thing she'd ever done to march that distance, as fast as her legs could carry her. By the time she reached the inn, she felt lightheaded with tension.

Nodding to the receptionist, who was engrossed in a magazine and barely raised her head, Mary made a beeline for the staircase, groping in her pocket for the key. Thank goodness it hadn't fallen out during her adventures.

She unlocked it, stepped inside, locked it behind her, and then, after some careful thought, took the chair from the dressing table and placed it under the handle.

Only then did she slump on her bed with a sigh of utter relief.

At least she'd made it here alive and with most of the folder's contents intact. One page near the back was missing, and she hoped it wouldn't prove to be vital.

Taking the folder from out of her jacket, she put it on the coverlet and stared at it, feeling scared and expectant all at once.

Someone had broken in, chased her, and had been ready to kill her for this. Although she had no idea who this person was, she knew from his height and build that he was an averagely sized man, and if she had to guess, she'd say his hair was dark.

"Now, I have to find out why you wanted this folder so badly," Mary muttered.

She undid the elastic bands and put them onto the nightstand. Then, she opened the folder marked Private, with a sense of expectation.

This was where the secrets she was searching for would be hidden. She was certain of it.

CHAPTER NINETEEN

As Mary paged through the Private folder, it took her a while to realize what these personal documents, belonging to the victim, were all about. The reason for that was that everything was in code.

Frowning in confusion, with page after page laid out on the bed, she revised her ideas that this was going to be simple and easy. It was going to be tough. And complicated. The original documents must all be filed away in a safety deposit box, she guessed. But what was in this folder was a careful list of names, and amounts, and dates.

Reading through, she slowly surmised that Harold Thompson had been a loan shark.

He'd specialized in giving loans of various sizes to people – from some of the jotted notes, Mary realized that some of the loans were for items as basic as farm machinery, others were for even larger purchases, like pieces of land. Some were to keep businesses ticking over during slow months, and others seemed to be for luxuries like horses or saddles. Or maybe, to the owners, those were necessities, Mary revised. At any rate, in these tough economic times, it seemed that Harold had done a roaring trade.

People who were hard up for money approached him, and he then loaned them the sum they required, at a considerable interest rate. Reading some of the monthly repayments, and doing mental arithmetic, Mary concluded that he'd been making a tidy profit on the repayments.

The papers were in chronological order, she realized, from the dates jotted next to each entry. Newest first. That meant that the page she'd lost while running was one of the older ones, probably from last year, or the year before.

What happened if they didn't pay?

Now thoroughly intrigued by the contents of the Private file, she paged on, trying to make sense of the jotted notes, and the coded comments.

If they didn't pay, it seems that Harold began issuing threats. He had even included a few standard letters, ready to fill in with the offender's name.

The threats ranged from minor, to very severe. And cleverly, Harold was using the village community as his bargaining tool.

Wide-eyed, she read one of the standard threatening letters.

"Dear ....," it began. *"You are thirty days behind on your repayments. That is unacceptable. Do you wish to be known in the village as a person who does not pay their debts? What kind of respect do you think people will have for you, if they discover you are a non payer, who defaults on their loans? If you wish to hold your head high in this village again, and not to have everyone talking about you behind your back, and laughing and sneering when your name is mentioned, suggest you make payment within forty-eight hours. If you do not, I will be forced to let slip the matter of your debt when I am next in the barbershop. Word will quickly spread, and I shall have no control over your destroyed reputation. And if that doesn't work, then I will have to take an advertisement in the local paper, to tell the whole community you are an untrustworthy person who is in bad standing.*

Yours sincerely, Harold Thompson."

Mary read and reread the threat.

"My goodness," she said aloud, casting an uneasy glance at the door.

This was a recipe for making enemies, if she'd ever seen one! Threats like these were dire! If somebody had by chance not had the money available, she could imagine the state of fear they would be in when they received this letter.

They would have been beside themselves, thinking of how their standing in the village would have been ruined.

Nobody deserved murder. That was very clear in Mary's mind. But at the least, she thought that Harold should have had a better imagination, and not considered himself to be invulnerable.

"Did you really think that nobody would figure out the best way to stop the threats, is by stopping the person who could make them?" she muttered. "At the very least, you should have hired a bodyguard."

No wonder he was so hated, and no wonder he despised the whole village the way he had done. It had come all the way down to pounds and pence and a contempt for those who took his loans.

Her mum had always said that money was the root of all evil, and this proved it.

"So," Mary muttered to herself. Since there was nobody else around – a fact that she was glad of right now after being chased – the only person there was to bounce ideas off, was herself. "What do I do now? I need to figure out which of his creditors killed him."

And now the problem was that there was a long, long list. He'd loaned money to hundreds of people throughout the county. At a rough guess, she thought that he had about thirty debts outstanding.

Thirty desperate people, any one of whom could have seized the opportunity to kill him at the summer gathering? That list was far too long for her to get through.

Would Constable Davies consider it as a lead?

Mary was dubious, especially seeing that a lot of the people on it were likely to be locals. And there was the next problem.

Although she went through the folder carefully, from beginning to end, there was not one place where Harold referred to any one of the creditors by their real names. He'd been far too cautious for that. Wherever the loan documents were – probably lodged in a bank's safety deposit box – they were not here.

And everyone had a code name, most of them to do with preserves.

There was Apple Sauce 10, there was Raspberry Jam 2, there was Crystallized Plum 25, there was Tangerine Marmalade 44.

Everyone had a code name! How on earth was she going to figure out the logic behind the codes, and also, which of all these creditors was the killer? Especially in the limited time she now had before either the police, or the killer, came looking?

Feeling agonized, she stared down at the pages, wondering where to start, and how she was going to find her way through the new, complex set of clues that this mean loan shark had left.

As she was frowning down at the page, a knock on the door almost made her jump out of her skin.

"Who – who's that?" Her heart was pounding. After her encounter earlier, she was not in the right mindset to handle sudden, loud noises. Glancing nervously at the chair, Mary wondered if it would hold up if it had to – and if there was a convenient drainpipe outside the inn's third floor window, if it came to that.

But her panic lasted only a moment before a voice filtered through from the other side.

"It's me!"

It was Hannah speaking, and never had Mary been so glad to hear her friend's voice. She rushed to the door, removed the chair, and unlocked it.

Hannah walked inside, staring curiously at Mary, then at the chair, and then at the piles of papers that were laid out on the bed.

"What's going on?" she asked. "You look - well, hunted." Moving quickly over to Mary, she grasped her hands. "Is everything alright?"

Mary sighed, squeezing Hannah's hands in turn, feeling her palms, hard and tough from the demands of her job, just as Mary's were. She noticed that Hannah was not wearing her maid's uniform but had changed into a dark green dress with a cream floral pattern. That must mean her Monday's work was over for the day. With a shock, Mary realized she'd spent far more time poring over these lists than she'd realized. The afternoon was lengthening into evening, and the killer was still out there.

"I was chased down earlier," she admitted. "Someone tried to run me down with their car, just as I was leaving the Beaumonts' estate."

Hannah goggled at her in horror. "Is that what happened to your bag? And where you got those cuts on your arms?"

"That's right," Mary said. "And then, when I was investigating Harold's house, the killer almost caught up with me again."

Hearing Hannah's gasp, Mary quickly continued. "I only just managed to get away. But I was able to find this folder, hidden in Harold Thompson's desk drawer. The killer came after it, too, wearing a mask. I was able to get into a house, and when he saw there were other people around, he left - fast. He's gone now. All I know is that he's a man, average height and build, and a very good runner. He nearly caught me."

She shivered again as she remembered that headlong pursuit and how she'd had to make life-saving decisions on the spur of the moment.

"Mary!" Hannah looked pale with shock. "That must have been terrifying!"

"It was. But this isn't over yet." Mary gestured to the papers. "You see, Harold was a loan shark, as well as being a nasty and critical jam judge. He loaned money to a lot of people in the neighborhood and beyond, charging high interest and with very strict terms. I think a lot of people would have ended up struggling to pay the money back."

"So what did he do?"

"He threatened them in destructive ways," Mary admitted. "He said that unless they paid, he'd destroy their reputation in the village, and I think he put terror into a lot of people. Nobody would have talked if they'd owed Harold money. Nobody would have wanted anyone else to know they had even incurred a debt like that – that they'd had to approach a local loan shark who was now forcing them to make high-interest repayments."

"But – but now you have this folder, won't the killer know? He must know his name is in here, and that you've taken the folder. That's why he chased you, right?" Hannah asked, frowning worriedly. "What if you never find out who he is? I mean, he might decide to leave town, or to – to move away and change his name, now that he knows you've got that folder."

"I don't think he'll do that," Mary replied.

"Why not?" Hannah asked.

"Because Harold was clever and cautious. He made sure that all the debts were listed in this folder under code names, so that only he would know who they were. And I accidentally dropped one of the older sheets, while I was running away."

Hannah was silent a moment, sitting on the bed, staring down at the pages.

"So, if the killer had picked up that sheet, then he would have seen that the names were all in code. And he would know that the police aren't going to come after him immediately?"

"Not immediately, no. He might think he's safe now and that I'll end up getting arrested after all. But he might also still want to kill me, just to make sure that his secrets never get found out." She glanced nervously at the door.

Having someone pursue her, twice, was nerve-racking enough for one day. Mary did not want to give this man a third opportunity.

"The police haven't arrested you yet, though?" Hannah asked.

"Not yet," Mary said. "But before I was fired by Lady Beaumont, she mentioned that Constable Davies had been called away to another village to investigate a theft incident. That's where he's been today. I don't think he's the fastest worker. But when he's finished up with the theft case, he'll come back. When he does, hearing that I was found in Maxwell's private study might be enough

Hannah shook her head, staring down at the pages in puzzlement.

"Jams?" she said in a questioning voice. "Did Harold really give jam code names to all the people he loaned money to?"

"Yes," Mary said. "There are pages and pages of names that relate to jams and preserves. I'm guessing he locked the original contracts away very carefully in a vault. He would not have wanted anyone destroying those, or he wouldn't have gotten his money back."

"And there's no record of where this vault might be?"

"None at all. Not in this folder. Even if he has a key for it, I doubt if the police would ever find out what the key unlocks, if it is one of a few on a bunch."

"You think he chose these code names randomly?" Hannah asked.

Mary glanced again at the pages. "Perhaps he didn't," she said. "If he had a system, we need to find out what it was, though."

Hannah bent down, taking a closer look at all the entries.

"They must have meant something to him. He must surely have used a system to decide on the code names, because otherwise even he might have gotten confused."

"Especially since he loaned money to a lot of people," Mary said.

Hannah nodded. "And nobody in the village is going to admit to this now," she said.

Mary shook her head. "Nobody who owes Harold Thompson money is going to say a thing. Why would they? The loan shark who was extorting high sums of interest from them, or from their friends and relatives, has been murdered. Everyone is going to keep quiet. That's why nobody in the village admitting to anything. It's a – a conspiracy of silence."

She stared at Hannah in desperation. Hannah grimaced.

"This is getting more and more complicated by the minute. I'm wondering if the only answer is to have some food," she said.

Despite herself, Mary grinned. Trust her friend to pick that solution to a problem. But she had to admit, she was starving.

"I suppose we'll be safe enough if we go down and get some food quickly?" she asked. "Especially now that this killer must know his name's in code?"

Hannah shook her head. "I still wouldn't risk it," she warned. "I think it's better if you stay here and guard the information, with a chair under the door, and I go out and get the food. When I come back I'll – I'll do a special knock. One tap, then two, then one again. Then you'll know it's me."

"Or you could just call out and say 'It's Hannah', like you did last time?" Mary pointed out.

Hannah blinked. "Yes. It's not quite as secretive, but yes, I suppose I could do that. Now, make sure you put the chair under the door when I leave, and get your thinking cap on."

"If we're going to figure out the secrets in this list, we're going to need to do it," Mary acknowledged. "Because I don't see Constable Davies cracking a code – or even thinking it's important."

"Especially not if Constable Davies is one of those who also owed Harold money," Hannah suggested darkly. "Then he might have a real interest in making sure it's never cracked.

And with that bombshell, she closed the door and left.

CHAPTER TWENTY

Feeling taut with worry, Mary began pacing the room again, her mind wrestling with the ways to solve what seemed like an unsolvable problem. A lot of people in the village were indebted to this unlikeable loan shark. One of them had murdered him, but nobody was going to say who. And the problem was that everyone had a vested interest in making sure Mary took the blame for it all.

Close-knit communities had their drawbacks, she decided, tensing as she heard footsteps approaching.

"It's me!" Hannah hissed.

Removing the chair from under the door, Mary let her friend in. Hannah must have gone down to the general store, because she'd come back with her arms piled high with convenience food.

Packets of peanuts, tubes of sweets, a slab of chocolate, a box of biscuits, and some packets of potato crisps, as well as two bottles of ginger ale.

It was by no means a conventional dinner, but Mary thought this quick and easy meal was perfect for their situation.

She replaced the chair under the door, just in case, while Hannah opened some of the food.

Mary took a shortbread biscuit, and munched on it thoughtfully.

"I think there are some assumptions we can make about who this killer is, apart from being a man of average height," she said.

"What are those?" Hannah asked, reaching for a potato crisp.

"I think he must have incurred a big debt recently and then run into trouble repaying it. There's obviously a strong reason why he didn't want Harold to name and shame him. Perhaps he has a reputation to protect, or his own business might be affected."

"And a larger amount would be more difficult to get the money for?" Hannah suggested. "If it was a small amount, then it would be easy to borrow the money or sell something to cover one of the repayments, wouldn't it?"

"Exactly," Mary said.

Taking a boiled, sweet, cherry flavor, she thought about what that meant. They were doing well in their deductions, and were definitely making progress, but the problem was that the field was still too wide. There were a few hundred people in this scenic village. To narrow down the killer's identity, they needed a name, and to do that, they somehow needed to crack the code.

Hopefully, the boiled sweet would give her the energy she needed to think this through.

She looked again at the names of the jams.

How had Harold assigned them? Had he gone by character? A squidgy jam for a squidgy person, a sour preserve for a sour personality? Did the numbers mean anything – could they relate to house numbers?

Shaking her head, she wished she had more information to use as a starting point. With no information, it was going to be a struggle.

"I'm wondering if anyone in the village would be willing to tell us?" Hannah suggested. Mary frowned dubiously.

"To tell us that they owed Harold money? What's the likelihood of that?" Hannah said.

"You're right," Mary agreed with a sigh. Unfortunately, in such a delicate situation, and especially after a murder, she didn't see anyone admitting to it.

She took a handful of peanuts and crunched on them, enjoying the saltiness, hoping that it would give her brain the energy it clearly needed.

"I was always bad at puzzles and word games," Hannah admitted, scratching her head.

"I have always been good at them," Mary said. "And I'm sure I can work this out."

Maybe she was looking at it the wrong way, she decided. It might be a better idea to assume that some of the people who'd been so evasive and angry to be questioned, had loaned money from Harold in the past, and to try to find their names on the list.

"I'm going to assume that Samuel was a customer," she said, taking a deep breath and focusing her mind. "He was so defensive when we questioned him, and so was Clara, his lover."

"The one thing we do know is that Samuel had an alibi," Hannah reminded her.

"Yes. But that defensiveness? Maybe he didn't want his secrets being told, and Clara knew it." Mary scanned the list, thinking hard.

"Samuel Blackthorn. What name would Harold have given him? How would he have linked it up to the real Samuel, so he could recognize it at a glance?"

These were important questions. And suddenly, staring down the list of names, she thought she had an answer.

"Strawberry Blend. That would be the same initials as Samuel Blackthorn?"

Hannah's eyes widened. "Maybe that's how he sorted them?" she asked.

"That would make sense?" With her finger on the list, Mary read down the columns. "In that case, Plum Jam might be – er – Percy Jones? Who runs the post office? I've heard his name in there." Mary had been to the post office twice to replace the stamps that she'd used to send letters to Gilbert.

"And Apple Preserves might be Adam Patricks. I know him – he owns an estate to the north of Beaumont Place. And I remember some of the other servants recently discussing the fact he'd invested in three new tractors," Hannah said excitedly.

"In that case…" Now, Mary had a particular set of initials in mind as she scanned the list, as well as the memory of that strange, secretive meeting that Maxwell Beaumont had had, on the first night he'd arrived.

"Mixed Berries! It has to be Maxwell! It has to!" With a rush of blood to her head, Mary realized that she'd managed to crack a key element of this case. No wonder Maxwell had looked so appalled when he'd found Mary in his office. He'd been worried that she would uncover the existence of this loan – a loan that Mary was now wondering if his mother even knew about.

If she hadn't known, that would be why Maxwell had wanted Mary out.

Hannah clapped her hands over her mouth in horror.

"You mean Maxwell was the killer? Mary, that's terrible!"

Mary hastened to correct her friend.

"No," she said. "I'm almost sure Maxwell is not the killer. He's one of the people I can rule out, because although I didn't see much of the car that tried to run me down, I saw enough of it to know that it definitely was not a white, low slung sports car like the one he drives. But that makes him even better for what I need, and that's information."

His mother hadn't known about the loan, and that gave Mary some bargaining power. Now that she knew which entry Maxwell Beaumont's was, she could use it to work out the killer's identity.

"Well," she said, "I might have been fired, but you and I need to go back to Beaumont Place now. It's time for me to have a conversation with Maxwell – and this time, on my terms."

CHAPTER TWENTY ONE

The afternoon was wearing on as Mary and Hannah walked back to Beaumont Manor. Mary felt encouraged that Hannah was with her. There was safety in having the two of them together – but mindful that the killer might be on the roads, they were taking the footpaths. They had gone out of the back of the inn, along a field, and were now on the farm track that led to the estate's small side gate.

Mary climbed over a stile to get in, handing the folder to Hannah as she did, and then took it back from her.

Against the darkening sky, the estate looked magnificent, its stone edifice elegant and stark against the blue and gold background. And behind her, Mary saw the village looked quaint and scenic, with lights starting to twinkle, nestled in the woods.

It was a shame to think that the entire village had been thrust into a state of fear, held captive by the money lender that had managed to get many people in his threatening grasp.

"Are you sure it's the right thing to bring the folder along?" Hannah asked.

Mary made a face. "I hope it is. The problem is that we really need Maxwell's help. And without the folder, he's not going to be able to help us."

"He could tear it up. He could throw it in the fire!" Hannah said.

"He can't throw it in the fire because there isn't one this time of year. As for tearing it up, that will take him a while," Mary said. "I think that between us, we can stop him from doing that if he tries."

Even though she was making sure to speak confidently, the truth was that nerves were surging inside her as she approached the house.

She was heading for the kitchen door, not the front door. Mary knew she needed to get inside unnoticed. Nothing must go wrong now.

Hannah went first, pushing the door quietly open before turning and beckoning Mary in. She tiptoed into the now quiet kitchen, and headed for the corridor, glancing around her as she walked. Everyone knew she'd been fired and banished from the premises. Anybody would be justified in calling Lady Beaumont if they saw her here.

They mustn't see her.

Checking before she walked into the main corridor, Hannah beckoned Mary to follow, and they tiptoed along. In another minute, they would be in Maxwell's wing. In another two minutes, they might know if this impromptu plan was going to work.

At least they'd managed to get inside without being seen. That was a big relief, Mary thought.

And just as she had that thought, she caught her breath.

Behind them, a door slammed. And Lady Beaumont's voice echoed down the corridor.

"Where is a maid when you need one? Why is nobody answering the bell?"

The voice was followed by the lady's distinctive footsteps, brisk and purposeful, approaching fast. The wrong Beaumont was homing in on them, and this could ruin everything.

"Hide!" Mary hissed to Hannah.

As one, they rushed to the only available hiding space – the closest door in the inconveniently long and bare corridor. Opening it, Hannah dived inside, with Mary following her. Mary nearly ended up on top of her. The door led to a musty-smelling linen closet. There was space for one small person – if they curled up tightly on the shelves. Now, two of them were trying to fit in a confined space that was already occupied by piles of sheets, pillowcases, down comforters, and warm woolen blankets that had all been packed away at the end of winter.

"Can you move over some more?" Mary whispered.

"Where?" Hannah whispered back, as Mary made a grab for the door, trying to pull it closed. "I can't get through the wall!"

Hauling on the door, Mary managed to pull it closed, crushing herself into the closet, and into Hannah. A shelf was digging into her shoulder. Hannah's knee was poking into her hip, the folder was jutting into her solar plexus, and a blanket with fluffy tassels was tickling her nose.

It was at that moment that Mary remembered mothballs always made her sneeze. And this closet was full of them.

She could feel the tickling worsening, and wrinkled her nose desperately, trying to keep the cupboard door flush with the wall as the footsteps approached.

The reason why Lady Beaumont had been unable to summon a servant, she realized, was because Mary would have been the one on late duty tonight. Clearly, in the excitement of firing her, she'd forgotten to replace her with anyone else on the roster. Now, she was reaping the rewards of her own actions.

"Where is a maid, for heaven's sake?" Lady Beaumont muttered.

If she only knew there were two just a yard away, breathlessly hiding in the closet. It would have been funny, if it had not been so fraught with peril. All the more since Mary knew she could not hold back her sneeze any longer.

The tickle was too extreme. Her nose was burning, her eyes were watering, she was going to have to sneeze, and then, standing so close by, the irate lady could not avoid hearing her.

Her shoulders were shaking, and her entire body tensing. Knowing that there was no way of holding it back, Mary could only resolve to do the most silent sneeze in the whole history of humanity – and mothballs.

But Lady Beaumont's sharp voice rang out again. "Oh, there you are, Stella! Thank you!"

At exactly the same time, Mary sneezed. Not as quietly as she'd hoped, and to make it worse, the sneeze caused the door to rattle. She and Hannah waited, frozen in apprehension, listening to the silence outside.

Visions of Lady Beaumont turning to the door suspiciously, flooded Mary's mind. She could almost see the lady giving it her eagle-eyed glare, wondering why it was faulty and making that rattling sound - and then pulling it open, to discover the cause was two terrified housemaids.

Or rather, one terrified housemaid, and one ex-employee.

But thankfully, frantic footsteps from down the corridor became louder, and Stella's apologetic voice rang out.

"I'm awfully sorry, m'lady. We never got around to changing the roster, so there was nobody on duty tonight. How can I help?"

"I'd like a cup of cocoa in my bedroom. I am retiring early. It's been a stressful week, and the cocoa will help me to sleep."

"Absolutely, m'lady. I'll get it for you right away. Would you like a little dash of brandy in it?"

"Yes. That will be a good idea. In fact, make it a large dash."

"I'll organize it."

The footsteps headed in different directions. One set back to the kitchen, and one set in the direction of Lady Beaumont's bedroom.

Mary sneezed again, and this time, the force of her sneeze caused the door to burst open and she tumbled out, rubbing her nose as she sprawled onto the polished wooden floor. Behind her, Hannah bundled out, closing the door quietly. She grabbed Mary's arm and pulled her in the direction of Maxwell's rooms, which were in the east wing.

"What was that sneezing all about?" she asked incredulously.

"Mothballs," Mary said. "They've always been a problem. They do something to my nose, and I – I can't stop myself."

She sneezed again. Already, the tickle was building once more.

"It's not going to be very intimidating for Maxwell if you're sneezing so badly we can barely threaten him," Hannah reprimanded her.

Mary's response was another sneeze.

"Oh, well," Hannah said resignedly. "At least we managed not to alert Lady Beaumont. I guess that's something. And here's Maxwell's rooms."

Ahead were the two doors that were familiar to Mary from this morning's chaotic events. The one on the left led to his bedroom. The one on the right was the study where she'd been fired. Mary was sure that the door would be firmly locked.

"Time to see if this will work," she breathed.

Lifting her hand, she knocked gently on the bedroom door.

CHAPTER TWENTY TWO

Footsteps sounded, causing Mary's heart to accelerate. Maxwell was inside, but he wasn't just letting anybody in by calling "Come in". He was checking the door. Suspicious already? She wondered what he'd do when he saw them standing outside. They might need to move fast if he tried to slam that door.

Maxwell flung open the door. He was wearing the smart black trousers that he must have dined in, but he'd taken off his dress shirt and was wearing a red and white striped pajama top. He stared from Mary to Hannah and back again, looking appalled.

"You were fired this morning!" he said in outrage, his gaze focusing on Mary. A whiff of wine-scented breath clued her that Maxwell might have indulged a little too freely in the aperitifs this evening. "What are you doing here? You were told to get out! To leave! I'm calling my mother!"

He took a deep breath, clearly intending to yell for her.

"Wait!" Mary said sharply, the word surprising him so much that he let the breath all the way out again. She wanted to follow up instantly with an authoritative statement, but unfortunately, what came out was an explosive sneeze.

Maxwell recoiled, taking a step back and staring at her suspiciously. "Do you have a cold?" he asked. "I don't want to catch your cold. I'm too busy doing my trading!"

"It's not a cold, it's…" Here, Mary had to pause to sneeze again. "It's hayfever," she continued. Finally getting to the gist of what she'd come here for, she pushed on. "We need to speak to you about something very serious."

"I don't care," Maxwell insisted, his face set in a stubborn glare. "You can speak to my mother along with me. I'm calling her now!"

"Does your mother know that you borrowed money from Harold Thompson, the recent murder victim?" Mary said very quickly.

His eyes widened. The aggressive tilt vanished from his chin. His eyes darted around in a way that told Mary he was thinking fast and furiously.

"You'd better come in," he said.

A moment later, she and Hannah were standing in Maxwell's spacious bedroom while he closed the door firmly behind them.

The bed was still made, and she guessed that Maxwell must have been preparing to climb into it when they arrived. His dress shirt was thrown over one of the arms of the plush leather couch near the window. He moved it, hanging it over the bed frame instead.

"Sit down," he said, indicating the couch. Mary and Hannah sat, and he took the chair by the desk, turning it to face them. The desk had a couple of documents on it, and a writing pad. It was clear that Maxwell really did take his work seriously.

Especially since, until very recently, he'd been paying back an expensive loan. Mary guessed that would motivate anyone to work hard.

"Look, how on earth did you find out about this?" he asked, with honest puzzlement in his tone. "I mean, this was all supposed to be confidential?"

"We have our ways," Mary said. Maxwell was no fool, though. He glanced at the folder.

"Yes, there's information in here," she admitted. "But it's not in a format you can read. Harold had a code system he used, and everything was encoded. The people who have loans are given fake names. I figured yours out because he uses the same initials."

"Well, why are you here?" Maxwell asked. Then, his gaze sharpened. "Look, you wouldn't be trying to blackmail me to get your job back, would you? Because let me say right now, I think that's unacceptable!"

"I agree," Mary said. "I wouldn't be doing anything like that. But since your mother doesn't know you borrowed from the local loan shark…"

"It was temporary!" Maxwell said defensively. "The markets moved against me, and one of my clients had to make an emergency withdrawal! I had no option but to borrow a – a bridging loan."

"Of course," Hannah said.

"And I didn't kill him! I'd actually just paid the loan back in full!"

So that was what that late night meeting had been about? It had been Maxwell, handing the cash to Harold. Probably, Harold had said something insulting, and that had caused the angry response Mary had overheard.

Mary opened the folder and found the name on the list that corresponded to Maxwell's.

"How much did you borrow?" she asked.

"You won't leak this to – to the local newspaper? I mean, I paid back my debt!" he protested.

"I promise I am not here to expose you, but it's very important for me to know this. Please tell me the truth," Mary said.

He sighed impatiently. "I borrowed ten thousand pounds."

Now, Mary was starting to see the light. The number ten, after his name, referred to the number of thousands he'd borrowed.

"And you paid it all back?"

"More's the pity, since someone killed him," Maxwell said ruefully. "I was so stressed about having to take that loan, it affected my entire life. I hate owing people money. Luckily, all it took was a few wise trades, and I'd made the loan back, plus his extortionate interest, plus a bit more to put aside in case any of my other clients decided they suddenly needed their funds. I paid in two installments. One last week, and one the night before the gathering."

And that would correspond to the two check marks next to his name. One check mark per installment. Harold's list was up to date, and he'd clearly checked that second amount off as soon as it had been paid.

"I mean, I didn't want him to mark my mother's jam down because I owed him money. But he did anyway," Maxwell said bitterly.

Mary was listening to this explanation – with half an ear. The rest of her attention was focused on the list.

If the number in front of the name indicated the size of the loan, then they had just obtained an extremely helpful lead.

Most of the numbers were relatively small. Two, three, ten, twelve. Mary guessed that the loan shark didn't deal in anything smaller than a thousand. He was after the high interest earned from lending out larger amounts, not in basic grocery money.

There was at least one check mark next to every name – most names had three or four of them as the lenders diligently paid back their inflated amounts.

But there was one number that stood out from the others. It was the only three-digit number. 242.

That was a lot of money. That was an excessive loan, and she could only imagine what the interest payments were. And there were no check marks next to that name. The borrower had never paid back a penny. Mary could imagine how furious Harold would have been about that. The threats that he'd issued must have been dire.

Faced with those threats, the borrower of the money had resorted to desperate action. At the fair, he'd decided to murder the lender so that his reputation would not be smeared.

That meant it was someone who desperately needed their reputation to be squeaky clean.

Looking at the name that Harold had given the man – Ginger Honey – gave her the final clue.

Now, Mary knew who the killer was. All she needed now was a way to trap him into a confession.

"I won't tell your mother," she said to Maxwell. "I can see why you wanted to keep this a secret. You needed to give a reliable impression to your clients, who wouldn't want to know you'd borrowed from a loan shark to bridge a gap."

"Exactly," Maxwell said.

"However," Mary said, raising a finger, "it so happens that I'm being wrongfully suspected of murder. I need to clear my name, and to make sure the real killer is caught."

Maxwell nodded thoughtfully. He seemed in a much more amenable frame of mind. Perhaps it had done him good to get that confession off his chest. And maybe he'd feel even better about himself if he got to do a good deed to atone for his rather childish behavior earlier today.

"I need your help to catch the killer," she said to Maxwell. "It would do wonders for your reputation if people knew you'd helped to catch him. A lot more people might choose to invest with you."

She could see Maxwell's eyebrows raising at that attractive thought.

"So," Mary said, "are you prepared to help us?"

There was a silence, broken only by the ticking of the small, gold clock on the mantelpiece. And then, Maxwell nodded decisively.

"I'm in," he agreed.

CHAPTER TWENTY THREE

Hiding behind a curtain was much more challenging than i sounded, even when it was one of the long, full, velvet curtains tha lined Lady Beaumont's drawing-room windows. There was an art to i Mary thought, as she tried to turn herself into a statue. You had to stan in a way that didn't interrupt the curtain's fall. You had to kee absolutely motionless.

And not sneezing? That was an imperative. At least these curtain didn't smell of mothballs.

Breathing quietly in and out, Mary tried to make herself one wit the wall and the window, doing her best to ignore the morning sun tha was streaming in, already making her hiding place uncomfortabl warm.

Nerves churned inside her. This was going to be a pivotal momen and she hoped that Maxwell would be a trusted ally. She didn't knov him well enough to be able to predict how he would handle thi pressured situation. Hopefully, as someone who traded on the stocl market, he was able to keep a cool head when things got stressful - because they might get stressful.

This killer would not capitulate easily. Not with so much at stake.

From the other side of the room, she picked up a tiny squeak Hannah was hiding behind the ornamental Japanese screen that wa placed at the southwestern corner of the room. The screen was slightl unstable, and the fact that it squeaked was not Hannah's fault. Mar hoped it didn't attract the killer's attention.

She needed him to be entirely focused on Maxwell until th moment came for them to show themselves.

A faint scratching of pen on paper was the only indication tha Maxwell was seated on one of the leather armchairs, with a noteboo on his lap, and a cup of coffee steaming beside him. Even behind th curtain, Mary could smell its rich aroma, gradually permeating th large room.

And then, from outside, she heard the noise she'd been waiting fc – the scrunch of tires on paving, as the car pulled up.

Mary knew what kind of car it would be. A big, dark car with a threatening looking grille and wide tires that had shredded a section of her travel bag.

The door slammed, and footsteps trod toward the front door. A moment later, the doorbell chimed.

She couldn't hear the muted conversation that followed, because the sound was drowned out by the grandfather clock, as it struck nine a.m.

"This way, sir," she heard the butler say, as the last chime rang out.

"Ah! So good to see you here!" Maxwell's voice rang out as the footsteps entered.

"Thank you for inviting me here and showing interest," the guest replied. Shivers ran down Mary's spine as she remembered this was the man who'd tried to run her down, and who had chased her, with intent to kill. He had everything to lose. She hoped that this would go smoothly.

"So tell me, Mr. Hopkins," Maxwell said. "I'd like to know more about these portions of land you have for sale."

Mary held her breath. How would he respond? Would he be willing to talk about the portions of land? Would he guess that this was a trap?

He didn't seem to be at all worried.

His voice sounded unconcerned, and as he spoke, Mary remembered the man, full of confidence, who'd been promoting his plots of land at the summer festival.

The small plots seemed to have been selling well, and they had been surprisingly cheap. There had certainly appeared to be a lot of interest surrounding them, but people had questioned why they were so affordable. Now, their cheap prices made sense. Mr. George Hopkins must have had the idea, from the start, that he was going to borrow a large sum of money to buy them, and then kill the lender, meaning that he would never have to pay back the money at all.

This was not a crime of passion, as she'd first thought, but rather, premeditated, and that made it all the more evil. With a shiver, Mary realized that he'd planned this, right from the time he'd begun advertising those plots. After all, with the dislikeable Harold having lent money to so many people, who would ever suspect him?

But Mary did. Thanks to figuring out the notes on that coded sheet, she knew that Hopkins was the worst of the non-payers. He'd never paid a penny, and had clearly stretched the time limit to its maximum before doing the deadly deed.

"How many plots do you still have available? Can you show me a map? Oh, and I'm being remiss. Would you like some coffee?" Maxwell was playing the part superbly, every inch the polite host.

"Coffee would be good." A chair scraped, and she imagined that Hopkins was sitting down. "Yes, they've been selling very well. Interest has been unprecedented. I've managed to keep a few of the prime ones on the north side, and those are now for sale – at a slightly higher price, but still way below what you'll pay anywhere else."

"Yes, these prices are incredible," Maxwell said. "How did you manage to keep them so low?"

That was the start of the trap. Mary held her breath.

"Wise buying," Hopkins – or Ginger Honey, as she was now thinking of him – said with satisfaction. "Sometimes, it's all about purchasing at the right time and then reselling when the market is ready. You're a man who trades in stocks. You should understand that, shouldn't you?"

"Yes," Maxwell said, still sounding confused. "I do trade in stocks, and that's why I find the price of your land to be quite impossible. I mean, I was wondering to myself whether you'd been given it, or inherited it? It seems like the only way to charge what you're doing for the stands themselves would be to be given the land for free."

That prompted an outraged gasp from Hopkins.

"Are you daring to doubt my credentials?" he snapped, and Mary's heart sped up. The mask was slipping.

"Merely asking about the tricks of the trade. There's no shame in owning inherited land. Ask me," he said wryly.

"I bought it wisely," Hopkins snapped. He was still thrown by the surprise question and by the fact that Maxwell had not accepted his story blindly.

Mary guessed most people had. After all when a deal was that good, people tended not to ask too many questions. And she was thoroughly impressed by Maxwell's performance so far. He'd been playing the part perfectly. It was strange how she'd changed her perception of him. From thinking he was an evil man who was a possible killer, she'd now realized that he was a trader who'd done his best for his clients, and had strived to help them.

He was far more ethical than she'd believed.

Maybe that was partly why he'd agreed to do this. She guessed that anyone with a shred of conscience would have been furious by what Hopkins had done.

"I didn't call you here to have an argument with you," Maxwell said. "I called you here to find out about the stands. But before you show me the map, I'd like to bring somebody else in. I'm not making this decision alone, you know."

There was a surprised pause. Then, clearly dredging up all the last reserves of his charm, Hopkins said, "Oh? Are you going to invite your good wife, or perhaps your fiancé, to be part of the process?"

Mary drew in a deep breath. Almost time for her part in this.

"Not exactly," Maxwell said. "There's somebody else who I think needs to be involved."

Just as she stepped out from behind the curtain, Hannah also stepped out from behind the screen. And, with a regal rustling of skirts, Lady Beaumont herself stepped out from behind the doorway that separated the drawing room from the dining room.

George Hopkins – or Ginger Honey – stared from one to the other to the third. And then, his face frozen, his gaze settled on Mary.

"You – you?" he choked out the words. "You?"

"Well, who else did you expect?" Mary asked. "I think we have some unfinished business, Mr. Hopkins."

"I – I don't know what you're talking about! I've never seen you before!" His face had turned a ghostly white, and he'd half-risen from his chair.

"I think you have. After all, you chased me the whole way down the road," Mary reminded him. "I was in fear of my life – although you were wearing a mask, it didn't conceal your intentions."

"You must have me confused with somebody else!" he blustered. "I was never at Harold Thompson's house!"

"How strange," Mary said, triumph flaring inside her. "I never mentioned Harold Thompson, or even which road I was in. You did. And I think you just admitted your guilt."

She stared at Lady Beaumont, who was watching her son with quiet pride. Then she stared at Hannah, whose eyes were wide and her expression as victorious as Mary felt inside. And finally, she turned her gaze to George.

He looked turned to stone, as if all the smooth talking in the world couldn't take back the words that he'd inadvertently uttered.

It seemed that he wasn't about to try to backtrack. Instead, with an expression of panic, he jumped from his chair, sending it clattering down behind him.

"Alright!" he shouted. "How much?"

"How much what?" Maxwell asked, pretending puzzlement in his tone.

"How much do you want as a share?" A ghostly mockery of a smile stretched his lips. "I admit, I was – well – reckless in my methods. I saw an opportunity to make a tidy pile by killing off the local loan shark who everyone hated. It was practically a public service! Nobody could say it was a bad deed. And the tidy pile exceeded my expectations. I guess, seeing you're all here, you could also do with a financial top-up."

Mary could not believe her ears. She gave Maxwell an astonished glance as the killer continued. "I'll be able to offer you – well, when I say 'you', I imagine you're working in two pairs? The Beaumonts and the housemaids? I'm happy to give each pair a total of fifty thousand tomorrow. It's more than fair. Trust me, it's a sizeable chunk of what I've made. But it's on the condition you say no more about it, do you hear? I guess any paperwork you have here, we can destroy and as for the rest – well, that idiot bragged that the contracts were held secretly, so I'm sure they'll never be found."

He stared around and his face turned even paler as he looked at Maxwell's expression, and then at Lady Beaumont's face, and finally, fixed his gaze on Mary.

"You tried to kill me!" Mary said. "Twice. You tried to run me down with your car, and then you chased me when you found I'd got to that folder first. You know full well that I'm the suspect in Harold's murder. Do you seriously think I'd take a portion of the – the obscene profit you made in exchange for keeping quiet about his death and confirming my own guilt?"

George was breathing rapidly, his chest rising and falling visibly.

"Alright," he said. "She's out. Are the rest of you in?"

"No!" Maxwell also rose to his feet. "We are not! This is nothing more than a conspiracy to cover up a murder, and I'm not prepared to be part of it. I'm an ethical man, and I hold myself to a strict code of conduct. What you've done is reprehensible. I hope you spend your life in prison!"

"Oh," George said, his gaze veering between them, "you needn't worry about that. I've made plans for that, you know, because I'm a thinking man, and I predicted that a catastrophe like this might occur if well-meaning do-gooders got involved. So, my last words are these – I have an exit plan! And you'll never find me!" Turning to Mary, he grinned. "I've written a full affidavit, delivered to the police station, saying that I saw you breaking into the victim's house, to try to find the threatening letter you sent him before the judging."

"What letter?" Mary asked, aghast.

"The letter that said if your employer didn't win the jam making competition, then you would kill him, because she'd promised you a bonus if you helped her win?"

"What?" Lady Beaumont said, her voice resonating with shock.

"I guess you didn't find it?" He smiled nastily as he chuckled. 'Don't worry. I'm sure the police will – and then, they won't look any further, will they? Who'd believe any of you, once that letter is in their hands?"

Mary sobbed in an astonished gasp. Now she knew why he'd broken in. it hadn't been to find the folder at all… it had been to incriminate her.

And he'd done it, masterfully.

Never had she thought she would be so effectively framed. That letter pointed the finger of guilt squarely in her direction, while also ensuring that the police would not believe a word the Beaumonts said.

Everyone knew, after all, how important that jam competition was.

"Well, sorry to be the bearer of bad news and all," he said cheerily. "But to convince the police you're the killer, I now have to leave. Adios!"

With a twist of his arms, he picked up his chair and flung it at Maxwell.

The chair whirled through the air, striking Maxwell a glancing blow on the head that sent him sagging to his knees. With a shattering of glass, a framed photo on the desk tumbled to the floor, and a vase crashed sideways, sending water streaming over the polished desk. And then, before Mary could process the shocking sequence of events, Ginger Honey had turned, and rushed out of the drawing room, heading unerringly for the front door.

The only sound was Maxwell, groaning as he tried to scramble to his feet. The chair had stunned him, and Mary thought one of the legs had caught him a serious crack on his temple.

"He's going to run for it!" she shouted. "We have to follow!"

From outside, the roar of an engine shattered the silence.

"Well, then," Lady Beaumont said in decisive tones. "Since my son is temporarily out of action, I suggest we follow him in the Range Rover. I refuse to let that odious liar get away. What nonsensical claims he made! I will not let him destroy my reputation – or yours, my dear."

Striding to the door, Mary and Hannah fell in behind her as the lady stopped, to grab a set of car keys from the side table, and then strode out, skirt swirling around her ankles, toward the Range Rover parked under an oak tree.

As Lady Beaumont clambered into the driver's seat, Mary flung herself into the passenger's side, opening the back door for Hannah who jumped in just as the car was starting up.

With the engine growling, Lady Beaumont reversed out of the parking space.

"Wall!" Mary called, realizing to her worry that the lady was being tardy in hitting the brakes.

With a jerk, the car stopped. With another jerk, Lady Beaumont got it into gear. And then, they were powering up the driveway in an alarmingly zigzag fashion, following the exhaust fumes that the fleeing killer had left behind.

CHAPTER TWENTY FOUR

"Gatepost!" Mary could hear the shrill horror in her own voice as the Range Rover veered up the driveway, gathering speed as it went.

"I will try my best to avoid it," Lady Beaumont replied in acerbic tones.

Gritting her teeth, Mary hung onto the seat and the dashboard respectively with her right and left hands, bracing her feet against the car's floor in the hope she might survive the inevitable impact.

Behind her, in a whisper, she thought she heard Hannah praying.

This cunningly contrived scheme had veered from certain victory all the way to disaster. George Hopkins had already had his exit plan in mind, and so far, it was succeeding brilliantly.

Of course, matters were handicapped by the fact that Lady Beaumont only looked to have been behind the wheel a handful of times in her life. Driving was clearly something that she left to her chauffeur.

She was up for the challenge – but what if she couldn't meet the challenge?

They shot past the gatepost, missing it by a hair's breadth. If Mary had stuck her nose out of the window, that nose would have been sheared right off. Then, clearly alarmed by the sudden need to change direction, Lady Beaumont fought with the wheel, while omitting to take her foot off the gas pedal.

"Right! Turn right!" Mary shouted, hoping that she could somehow encourage the car around the turn by the power of her voice alone.

"I am about to!" Lady Beaumont chastised.

She was about to go into the hedge on the other side of the road. By a miracle, the car managed to swing away at the last minute, taking the hairpin turn on two wheels as Mary held her breath.

Gathering her wits, she did her best to overcome her fear, and stared ahead. There was a strong likelihood that George would get away. Someone who'd planned so meticulously would have a well crafted exit plan, and he had the money to execute it.

If he got out of the village, he could go anywhere. Bus, train, even ship or airplane. He might have managed to get a different passport. He could live his life in the lap of luxury in a different country or continent.

And what would happen to her?

With the perpetrator fled, Constable Davies might decide that the village needed somebody in custody, and that somebody would be her. Trouble was still hanging over her, like a stubborn raincloud that refused to move.

"He turned right here!" Staring intently at the upcoming crossroads, with quaint wooden signs pointing the way to various villages, Mary had caught a glimpse of George's car above the hedge. He was gaining ground. That wasn't hard, because with Lady Beaumont's driving, she was wasting double the time in zigzagging from hedge to hedge.

If they met an oncoming vehicle, the result would be carnage. Mary prayed that at this quiet hour of the morning, nobody would be out and about.

Where was he going? The hedges on each side were thick and solid. She knew this because the veering Range Rover occasionally removed a few solid twigs from them, with a screaming sound that had Hannah gasping.

"I think he went right here!" Mary said.

"Nonsense, my girl! I was keeping an eagle eye out, and he most definitely turned left," Lady Beaumont said, veering around the turn and missing the signpost by a mere inch.

Then, Mary's worst nightmare started to play out. As they hurtled down the narrow lane, with no sign of George's car ahead, what they did see was an oncoming vehicle.

Lady Beaumont gave no indication that she had seen it. It was almost as if she was in a trancelike state.

"Um, my lady," Mary said, in a shaking voice. "I think you need to slow down!"

White knuckled, Lady Beaumont's hands gripped the wheel. But where were her feet! The foot on the brake was what Mary was hoping for.

"Stop!" Hannah yelled from the back seat, and Lady Beaumont jumped at the sound. As if it had jolted her out of her thoughts at last, she mashed her foot on the brake.

"Why didn't you tell me earlier?" she asked irritably.

Mary was watching the car's oncoming grille. It was approaching a lot too fast. Would the Range Rover manage to avoid it? The other driver had already braked sharply, burying the car's nose in the hedge to avoid a catastrophic crash. But with Lady Beaumont's lack of control, that might still happen.

The Range Rover rocked to a stop, just as its grille touched the left side bumper of the car facing it.

In a flood of realization, Mary realized she knew that car – and its driver. It was Gilbert!

In the nick of time, he had arrived.

"I'll go with him," she said, leaping out of the driver's seat and slamming the door behind her. In a moment, she'd bundled in beside Gilbert.

"What's happening?" he asked, sounding puzzled.

"We're chasing a killer," Mary said in firm tones.

Gilbert raised his eyebrows. "A killer?"

"Go that way." She pointed ahead.

Gilbert swerved sharply, veering into the hedge to get past the Range Rover's bulk. And then, they sped off up the hill, toward the turning that Mary suspected the car had taken.

"I suppose things escalated while I was away?" Gilbert asked.

"They did. We trapped the killer with the help of the Beaumonts. But he made a run for it," Mary said. "If he gets away, it's back to square one. Constable Davies might believe the Beaumonts, but he might also think that he needs to get a suspect in custody for the sake of his reputation. How well do you know the roads around here?"

"Not as well as a local," Gilbert said worriedly. "But I'll do my best. Which way here?"

It was now down to guesswork, but as Mary made the decision, she caught a glimpse of the fleeing car, about a mile away and traveling fast.

"Lef- no! Right! Right! He's going down toward Chelston!"

"Then so am I!" Gilbert swung the wheel in that direction, operating his car with a thousand times more dexterity than Lady Beaumont had done. He sped down the road, judging each turn finely, yet safely. And now, the runaway vehicle was coming into view again.

"I think we have him! I think we do!"

Triumph resounded in Gilbert's voice as he saw what was appearing beyond the Range Rover.

A massive tractor blocked the way. In fact, as Mary's astounded mind put two and two together, she realized it was one of the fleet of tractors from the neighboring estate.

The tractors that the owner must have bought with a high-interest loan from the victim himself. How fitting that it was now blocking the way.

Tires screeched as George's car braked, veering left and right as he tried to find a nonexistent way out. And then, the car reached a standstill. George jumped out, desperation evident in every line of his body. In a final, last-ditch attempt to escape, he bolted toward the hedge.

He was a fast runner, but Gilbert was faster. In a flash, he leaped out of the car and raced in George's direction, gaining ground on him with every stride. Mary held her breath as Gilbert launched himself into a flying tackle.

Too soon, she thought, with a lurch of her heart. Too soon. He was going to miss.

But as he flew through the air, Gilbert's outstretched hand snagged the tails of George's coat.

He stumbled, his ankle twisting under him, and hit the ground heavily.

With a thud, he landed, and the next moment, Gilbert was on him, wrestling his hands behind him as Mary ran up to help.

"Got any rope?" Gilbert called to the tractor driver with a pleasant smile, leaping aside to dodge George's flying elbow.

"It's for a good cause!" Mary echoed. "Catching a criminal who was about to escape!"

The next moment, a coil of rope landed on the road next to Gilbert's elbow.

As he efficiently trussed the writhing, shouting suspect, Mary felt a sense of relief fill her.

A killer had been caught – and despite a nasty twist of circumstances, and cunningly planted evidence, Mary herself was going to walk free.

CHAPTER TWENTY FIVE

"I'm so relieved you were there! You saved the day," Mary said.

Sitting next to Gilbert in his car, she was watching the heartwarming sight – to her, anyway – of a shouting and protesting George Hopkins being loaded into the police van.

"No," Gilbert said. "You saved the day! If it hadn't been for your investigation, then that man's planted evidence would have sunk you." He sighed. "You know, Mary, I've always been worried when you've started investigating – I can't help it. I get concerned for your safety, and I start thinking of all the things that could have gone wrong – but if you hadn't investigated yourself this time, then it would have been a total disaster."

"It might not have ended well," Mary said. "The problem is, you see, that people don't believe the word of a housemaid. I've seen it happen time and again."

"It's an unfair and unequal world," Gilbert agreed somberly. "And it's people like you, who understand that inequality and still fight for justice – and do so with a sense of humor, too – who are the people I most respect."

That made Mary feel warm inside. And she liked it that Gilbert had praised her sense of humor. It was one of the qualities that Mary felt seldom let her down or abandoned her.

"I guess we should be getting back," she said. "Lady Beaumont has invited us all to dinner."

When the Range Rover had pulled up, shortly after the police arrived, with a few dents in the hood, and a sheet-white Hannah on the back seat, Lady Beaumont had been full of apologies.

"Mary and Hannah," she'd declared, "I misjudged you, and have been forced to confront the error of my ways. Please join me and my son tonight – not as our workers, but as our guests, for dinner, bed and breakfast."

"I'd love to," Mary said, glancing at Gilbert.

"And of course, your young man is invited, too," Lady Beaumont said, giving Gilbert a gracious smile.

It was a first time for Mary. She'd tidied countless rooms in country houses, she'd made hundreds, perhaps even thousands of beds. Cooking, plating, and serving were all part of her skills. But never before had she actually sat at a table in a grand country house while dinner was being served.

This was a shock turnaround, but she was looking forward to it.

"I guess, at last, I'll get to see how the other half live," she said to Gilbert wryly, as he started up the car and drove back to Beaumont Place.

***

The moon was bright and yellow in the sky. A smell of night scented jasmine hung in the air, and from somewhere, Mary could hear the soft calls of an owl.

It felt like an enchanted evening. The two Beaumonts, Gilbert Hannah and Mary had enjoyed a delicious three course meal of asparagus, partridge confit, roast potatoes, and berry crumble, with more than one glass of fine wine to wash it all down. Conversation had flowed. Both Lady Beaumont and Maxwell had apologized for ever having doubted her, and Maxwell had explained, in a shaking voice, that he was still mourning his father, and realized that his behavior was inappropriate at times.

Mary, in turn, had talked about the death of her mother, and in strange way, she thought that speaking about that had offered the Beaumonts some comfort. They'd all ended up toasting their love ones, and at the end of the dinner, everyone had hugged each other fondly before going their separate ways.

What an experience! She felt pleasantly tired, and ready for her bed in the fine bedroom that was known as the Rose Room, because looked out over the rose gardens.

"I haven't had a chance to talk to you recently," Gilbert said, "about the future."

There was an edge in his voice that hadn't been there a few minutes ago, but what with the wine and the excitement of the day, Mary didn't notice anything unusual about it.

"Well, my future's up in the air," she said. "Because you see, when we got back, Hannah received a letter from the man she met when we were on holiday. He said there's an opening at the hotel next door to him

– for an assistant manager. He's recommended her, and they're willing to take her on and train her for the job."

"Are they?" Gilbert asked, still with that strange note in his voice.

"She didn't want to accept the job, because it was for her alone, rather than the two of us," Mary said. "But I told her not to be silly. It's an opportunity she can't pass up. She could go on to great things. Hannah could easily be the manageress of a hotel one day. We can stay friends and see each other whenever we can. So that's all sorted. But as for me, well, there's that invitation I had from the detective. I've been thinking about it so much, and I have decided it's the right thing for me. I just need to figure out where I'll stay, and –"

Suddenly, it struck her that Gilbert's demeanor was decidedly nervous. A thrill of anticipation tingled inside her as he turned to face her, with an expression more intense than she'd ever seen before.

"Mary Adams, if there's one thing that the past few months have taught me, it's that life with you is an unstoppable adventure," he said. "It's an adventure I want to continue – with you. And I'd like to make a suggestion. That you come back to the lodge house at my estate. It's beautiful, it's cozy, and it will be yours and mine. I know I'm busy some of the time with my business, and you're going to be busy with your detective work. But the rest of the time – we'll have each other. And that would delight me more than anything I can think of."

Her mouth dry, Mary nodded, as he took her hand in his.

"I feel the same, Gilbert. We've had so many adventures together in such a short time, and I've loved every one of them. But I think we're owed some of the time between, some of the ordinary time."

"Exactly. To sit with a cup of tea, or do some gardening together, or go for lovely long walks, or admire a sunset?"

"Yes. Those times. The times that I've dreamed of spending with you, and wished we could have a thousand times over," she said.

His hand was holding hers tightly as he looked into her eyes. Leaning forward, he kissed her so tenderly that a million butterflies took wing inside her. The kiss seemed simultaneously to last forever, and not nearly long enough.

As he stepped away, stroking her face, she heard a quiver in his voice as he continued.

"Since we both want the same thing, I'd like to propose – well, a proposal. I'd like to offer you – oh, good heavens, I'm doing this so badly!"

Suppressing a giggle of pure delight, feeling her heart speed up, she watched in astonishment as Gilbert, still holding her hand, dropped clumsily to his knees while digging in his pocket. She'd never believed that something so romantic, and touching, and special, and endearingly flawed would play out in her life, never mind tonight.

"Mary, I love you," Gilbert declared, producing a velvet box. He opened it to reveal a sparkling diamond ring, nestling on the dark blue cushion inside. "Forever with you will never be long enough – so let's make a start. Will you marry me?"

NOW AVAILABLE!

A MYSTERY IN BLOOM: MURDER IN THE MARIGOLDS
(An Alice Bloom Cozy Mystery—Book 1)

For landscape designer Alice Bloom, plants are more than just her job—they are her passion. But her latest project turns grim when a despised socialite is found dead in an Italian villa's garden—and Alice, finding herself blamed for the crime, has no choice but to solve it herself.

Drawing on her own extensive botanical knowledge, Alice must dig through the layers of aristocratic secrets and intrigue to unearth the killer, and to clear her name before it's too late. But a new romance may just have her distracted with other things…

A Mystery in Bloom: Murder in the Marigolds (An Alice Bloom Cozy Mystery—Book 1) is the first novel in a new series by cozy mystery author Fiona Grace.

The Alice Bloom series is a page-turning, charming cozy mystery that invites you into a picturesque setting, packed with humor, romance, and surprise twists and turns. You'll be up well past bedtime as you fall in love your new favorite female protagonist.

Future books in the series are also available!

Fiona Grace

Fiona Grace is author of the LACEY DOYLE COZY MYSTERY series, comprising nine books; of the TUSCAN VINEYARD COZY MYSTERY series, comprising seven books; of the DUBIOUS WITCH COZY MYSTERY series, comprising three books; of the BEACHFRONT BAKERY COZY MYSTERY series, comprising six books; of the CATS AND DOGS COZY MYSTERY series, comprising nine books; of the ELIZA MONTAGU COZY MYSTERY series, comprising nine books (and counting); of the ENDLESS HARBOR ROMANTIC COMEDY series, comprising nine books (and counting); of the INN AT DUNE ISLAND ROMANTIC COMEDY series, comprising five books (and counting); of the INN BY THE SEA ROMANTIC COMEDY series, comprising five books (and counting); of the MAID AND THE MANSION COZY MYSTERY series, comprising five books (and counting); of the ALICE BLOOM COZY MYSTERY series, comprising five books (and counting).

Fiona would love to hear from you, so please visit www.fionagraceauthor.com to receive free ebooks, hear the latest news, and stay in touch.

A SPEAKEASY DEMISE (Book #4)
A FLAPPER FATALITY (Book #5)
BUMPED BY A DAME (Book #6)
A DOLL'S DEBACLE (Book #7)
A FELLA'S RUIN (Book #8)
A GAL'S OFFING (Book #9)

LACEY DOYLE COZY MYSTERY
MURDER IN THE MANOR (Book#1)
DEATH AND A DOG (Book #2)
CRIME IN THE CAFE (Book #3)
VEXED ON A VISIT (Book #4)
KILLED WITH A KISS (Book #5)
PERISHED BY A PAINTING (Book #6)
SILENCED BY A SPELL (Book #7)
FRAMED BY A FORGERY (Book #8)
CATASTROPHE IN A CLOISTER (Book #9)

TUSCAN VINEYARD COZY MYSTERY
AGED FOR MURDER (Book #1)
AGED FOR DEATH (Book #2)
AGED FOR MAYHEM (Book #3)
AGED FOR SEDUCTION (Book #4)
AGED FOR VENGEANCE (Book #5)
AGED FOR ACRIMONY (Book #6)
AGED FOR MALICE (Book #7)

DUBIOUS WITCH COZY MYSTERY
SKEPTIC IN SALEM: AN EPISODE OF MURDER (Book #1)
SKEPTIC IN SALEM: AN EPISODE OF CRIME (Book #2)
SKEPTIC IN SALEM: AN EPISODE OF DEATH (Book #3)

BEACHFRONT BAKERY COZY MYSTERY
BEACHFRONT BAKERY: A KILLER CUPCAKE (Book #1)
BEACHFRONT BAKERY: A MURDEROUS MACARON (Book #2)
BEACHFRONT BAKERY: A PERILOUS CAKE POP (Book #3)
BEACHFRONT BAKERY: A DEADLY DANISH (Book #4)
BEACHFRONT BAKERY: A TREACHEROUS TART (Book #5)
BEACHFRONT BAKERY: A CALAMITOUS COOKIE (Book #6)

CATS AND DOGS COZY MYSTERY
A VILLA IN SICILY: OLIVE OIL AND MURDER (Book #1)
A VILLA IN SICILY: FIGS AND A CADAVER (Book #2)
A VILLA IN SICILY: VINO AND DEATH (Book #3)
A VILLA IN SICILY: CAPERS AND CALAMITY (Book #4)
A VILLA IN SICILY: ORANGE GROVES AND VENGEANCE
(Book #5)
A VILLA IN SICILY: CANNOLI AND A CASUALTY (Book #6)

ALICE BLOOM COZY MYSTERY
MURDER IN THE MARIGOLDS (Book #1)
RUIN IN THE ROSES (Book #2)
DECEIT IN THE DAFFODILS (Book #3)
SCANDAL IN THE SAFFRON (Book #4)
CATASTROPHE IN THE CARNATIONS (Book #5)

Made in the USA
Las Vegas, NV
29 April 2024

89320544R00090